Brine and Bone

Other Works by Kate Stradling

The *Annals of Altair* Series:
A Boy Called Hawk
A Rumor of Real Irish Tea

The *Ruses* Series:
Kingdom of Ruses
Tournament of Ruses

Goldmayne: A Fairy Tale

The Legendary Inge

Namesake

Brine and Bone

a Novella

Based on H.C. Andersen's
"The Little Mermaid"

Kate Stradling

Eulalia Skye Press
MESA, ARIZONA

Brine and Bone

Copyright © 2018 by Kate Stradling
katestradling.com

All rights reserved. No part of this book may be reproduced or transmitted in any form or by any means, electronic or mechanical, including photocopying, recording, or by any information storage and retrieval system, without written consent of the author.

Published by
Eulalia Skye Press
PO Box 2203, Mesa, AZ 85214
eulaliaskye.com

ISBN: 978-1-947495-02-9
Library of Congress Control Number: 2017919456

For Cai and Camden,
two charming princes who love
the creatures of the deep

Preface

Stop. If you're expecting a clone of a certain redheaded underwater songstress who trades her voice for a three-day gamble to win true love, prepare for disappointment. While that famed revision provides the heroine her happily ever after, it also murders the original narrative.

I've long held a fascination for "The Little Mermaid" in its first incarnation, particularly its jarring end. Sea foam? Wind spirits? What was Andersen thinking?

But he was thinking something. (Writers typically do.) Every time I encounter a new incarnation of this story, while I might enjoy the rewrite, a buried part of me whispers, "That's not how it really happened."

Is revisionist storytelling any better than revisionist history? Do we as authors serve our readers best when we shelter them from painful truths?

Is it even possible to rewrite "The Little Mermaid" and stay faithful to its original ending without suffering the wrath of the jilted reader?

We're about to find out.

For years I muddled over how to approach this tale without completely alienating my audience, only to realize that the answer has been staring me in the face.

So I've put it to the test, and now you get to be the guinea pig. (Providing you didn't shut the book after the second sentence of this preface, of course.)

Many thanks to my beta-readers, Edith Stradling, Kristen Ellsworth, Chris Rhoton, and Rachel Collett. There may have been others. Sometimes my drafts get passed around. Thanks, also, to Claire and Cai, who listened faithfully, and to Camden, who tried.

Finally, thanks be to God, the true source of inspiration, who revealed the surprisingly simple answer to my conundrum.

It was all a matter of perspective, you guys.

K.S.
January 2018

Prologue

EVERYONE LOVED THE CROWN PRINCE of Corenden. An only child spoiled rotten by his noble parents, he somehow developed a charming personality to match his handsome face. He offered kindness to everyone he met, with a smile that could curl even the grimmest mouths upward.

I say that everyone loved him, but I mean that everyone loved him except for me. I worshiped the ground he walked on and hated him for it.

He belonged to us all, our future king. We knew that one day he would marry a lady of the realm or a princess from a foreign ally but he would never truly be hers. I couldn't imagine him being anyone's. He treated noble and peasant alike with the same respect, never gave preference to one person over another, always a peacemaker. In our younger days, when the girls of the court would fight over who could sit next to him or who could play with him, he would gently chide them. He only chided me once, and I never fought over him again.

He never let me live it down, either.

There were so many young ladies at court. Half of us didn't even belong to Corenden proper. The older generation schemed, and we remained oblivious, so young when we arrived that we had no thought beyond playing with one another in the sunlit gardens and along the glittering shore. Our parents hoped the prince would develop feelings for one of us, that they might secure the royal lineage through the bonds of childhood friendship.

He never did and, somehow, all the girls at court knew he never would. It was the way he spoke of his future wife: "Someday I'll marry and bring her home with me, and we must all be friends together."

We knew she didn't exist among us. Some of the girls swore we would have a fairy for our next queen, for surely no mortal could merit the good-natured boy.

They still bickered and bargained, though.

On one such occasion, they struck a sound piece of logic. "If we're all to be friends, she won't begrudge us your favor. Come walk with us to the sea, your Highness."

But he only shook his head. "I can't come unless everyone goes. Magdalena's stuck in her books again."

The sound of my name drew my brief attention. I quickly retrained my gaze upon the weathered pages, though the words danced before me now like insects in a flower garden, erratic and unintelligible.

"Magdalena's always stuck in her books. She won't care if we go without her."

"She will care. I don't want to upset her like I did before."

The remark earned him the scowl he sought from me. He returned it with his charming smile and I fought the fluttering blush that stole from my heart to my cheeks. "I don't care if you go without me," I said, snapping my book shut and tucking it under my arm. "I won't be here for much longer anyway."

And I wasn't. At twelve the threads of magic that had often sparked around me tightened into a knot of inborn ability. The king and queen wrote my parents, who had no choice but to remove me for proper training at the sage's seminary further up the coast.

Thus my time at the court of Corenden ended as abruptly as it began, and I committed its halls and its charming prince to my memories. For six years I worked and studied and matured. Stories of the court, of the prince and his shimmering entourage, flitted through the seminary as they did through every other part of the kingdom. The prince grew in height and charm, and his admirers multiplied into the thousands. When he toured the countryside with his father, his people lined the roads to catch a glimpse. When he passed through cities, they showered him with rose petals. When he sailed to visit the northern islands, they crowded the docks to bid him fond farewell.

And when word arrived that his ship had sunk in a storm, and that the merciless waves had torn him from the lifeboat into their briny depths, the people mourned as a nation struck with monumental grief.

And I shut myself in my bedroom and sobbed until exhaustion dragged me to sleep.

Chapter One

THICK FOG ENSHROUDED THE SHORE. It diffused the dawn sunlight into somber gray and deadened the roar of the receding tide to a murmur. The thready wind shifted it against a gaggle of robed young women, who drew their flowing garb closer in the clammy chill.

"Magdalena! Magdalena, you're going the wrong way!"

A hissing voice quickly silenced the shrill first. "Shh. Leave her be to wander."

"But, Master Demsley said—"

"Master Demsley will understand. It's a miracle we got her out of bed this morning."

"But—"

"Worry about yourself, Renae. Magdalena will be fine."

Magdalena shut her ears to the conversation and trekked further from the group. The pair of voices and the shadowed silhouettes to whom they belonged moved deeper into the clouded mist, until she could hear nothing of them. The fog around her cut her off from everything except this patch of sandy earth on which she stood, as though nothing else existed in the world.

Would that that were true.

Her head ached. Her brown hair, pulled tight into a braided bun, made the throbbing worse. She rubbed at one temple, her gritty eyes fixed on the beach as she trudged across its misted length. The group had come in search of ingredients most readily found when the tide went out, and she knew she ought to help with the gathering.

She ought to, but she wouldn't. Master Demsley had only wanted her out of her room. He had told her himself that no one would blame her if she chose to vacate the seminary for a few days or more.

By now all the girls would know what a stupid fool she was. They all mourned, stricken when the news came with the evening courier. Magdalena, however, had taken it as a mortal blow.

"I don't understand. She was never even interested to watch when he passed through the village."

"She knew him, you dummy. They were friends when they were children."

The whispered voices had plagued her all night, her magical senses aflame in the hours of her grief. The pain of her schoolmates—shallow, superficial pain though it was—worked her into deeper despair, like sandpaper rubbed against a torn and angry wound.

Yes, she had known him ages ago, in a part of her life that seemed more like a dream than reality. Here on the misty shore she could pretend that memory didn't exist.

Pretend, but never really believe. Her heart ached more than her head.

The cliffs loomed to her left, monstrous shadows. She skirted closer to them as the sand gave way to pebbles and the shore narrowed. The clammy rocks provided her something to lean on as she progressed. The beach would widen again further up, in a small cove, an isolated spot where she could wallow in her misery. At the narrowest point of the passage, the gray sea churned foam against her boots, licking the soles, inviting her into its cloudy depths.

Magdalena scowled and moved on. Just because the crown prince had met his death in the ocean didn't mean she was duty-bound to follow. She resented him for the morbid desire even flitting through her mind.

Yet another resentment to add to her growing list.

By the time she passed the rocky strip, the fog had thinned. The sheltered cove stretched before her, the vegetation at its edges mere dollops of green within the mist. Debris littered the sand in dark, hunched shapes, as though the sea had attempted a sluggish assault upon the land. Seaweed and driftwood cluttered her path. The waves here, smaller, lapped gently against the slick sand. Magdalena paused to breathe the salt-heavy air. She closed her eyes and drank in the solitude of the remote beach.

Plash, plash, plash.

She matched her breath to the rhythm of the shore until—

A chitter and a sploosh jarred her senses. Her eyes flew open and her hand moved to the knife at her waist—a knife meant for cutting potion ingredients, but a weapon nonetheless. The fog, still dissipating, concealed the source of the animalistic noise. Magdalena swiveled, her spine crawling with apprehension, but nothing more than driftwood occupied the shore with her. The creature—whatever it was—had moved to the ocean rather than the shrubbery further inland.

When no additional sounds followed, she eased herself from her defensive stance. Still her breath caught in her throat with every inhale. Her skin prickled a warning: something was watching her. The waves rolled across the small cove from a distance still obscured. She reached out not with her physical senses, but with her magical ones.

In reply, exhaustion seeped into her bones.

She clapped that avenue shut as she staggered to one side, her head reeling with images of roiling waves and a bright, beating sun. A knot tightened her windpipe. Again she searched the cove, desperate to find the source of this errant, destructive empathy. She stumbled in the sand, catching herself before she could fall. Her vision danced in triplicate but resolved as she focused on a large, slumped piece of driftwood further up the shore.

Not driftwood.

Human.

The word pulsed through her brain. Adrenaline spiked in her blood, and she pushed forward into a run, kicking up sand as she closed the distance. If she could sense such feelings, the castaway wasn't dead.

Perhaps it was—

If only—

She tamped down hope as she skidded to her knees beside the sodden figure, but it bubbled up her throat again with a sob.

The dark hair plastered against a stubbly jaw could not hide the familiarity of a face she had tried for ages to banish from her mind.

The crown prince of Corenden, claimed by the merciless ocean two nights ago, had washed ashore. He was not dead.

Yet.

Magdalena's years of training engaged. "Your Highness," she said, turning him to lie on his back. "Your Highness, can you hear me?"

She leaned close to listen to his shallow breath. Her magical senses probed for the nature of his injuries.

Sunburn. Dehydration. Bruises. Remnants of saltwater in the lungs and a lump half the size of her fist on the back of his head.

Phantom pain burst upon her skull, coupled with images of a tossing ocean and crashing debris. As the lifeboat lowered into the water that night, a piece of the ship had struck his head, pitching him into the deep. She caught her breath and tempered the vision, her gaze huge upon the prince.

It was a miracle he had not sunk to the bottom of the ocean and stayed there.

She fumbled with the medical bag she always carried—the bag that healing magicians, by law, had to keep with them—grateful that she had thought to slip it over her head before leaving her room an hour ago.

The Prince was alive.

The Prince was alive.

Her hands shook. She extracted a vial of smelling salts and almost dropped it when she unstopped the lid. She waved it toward his nose, heard the sharp inhale and—

That spine-chilling chitter sounded from the waves.

Her attention snapped to the rippling ocean, where the fog thinned to reveal sullen, iron-gray waters.

Bulbous eyes stared back at her, set into a slick, silvery head. Her brain struggled to match this image to a familiar beast. A seal, perhaps? Pale in color, or rendered so by the fog around it?

Magdalena peered at the creature. It remained motionless, frozen in place, unaffected by the waves that steadily trundled around it. The marbled eyes did not blink. Her own watered and blurred. The longer she looked, the stranger the creature appeared. The silver of its head seemed to bleed into the water around it, like weeds clinging upon a reef.

It eased up from the ocean an inch, revealing a sloped bridge of bone devoid of nostrils. Magdalena's pulse galloped in her throat. Another two inches revealed full lips and the jumbled, pointed cross-bite of a deep-sea creature—those elusive monsters that fishermen sometimes snared and brought home to frighten "landlubbers."

The sharp teeth parted, as though the silvery creature would speak.

A groan much nearer invoked a shriek from the startled girl. The salts dropped from her limp grasp, and she focused on her patient again.

The prince's eyelids fluttered. She moved to place a soothing hand upon his brow. "Your Highness?"

A splash drew her glance oceanward once more. The creature with the marbled eyes had vanished into the brine.

The prince groaned again, his voice like a frog. With the mystery observer gone—for now—Magdalena gave him her undivided attention.

"Don't try to talk. Don't move. You need water and medical care."

His gray eyes—the color of the sea—focused on her face. She fought a self-conscious blush and rummaged around in her bag for the small flask she always carried with her. Suddenly she didn't know how to speak with this man.

She had spent all of last night mourning his death, as though they had been the most intimate of friends.

He probably couldn't pick her face out of a crowd. Why should he remember a girl who left his court when they were both still children?

And yet, "Magdalena." Her name left his lips on a whisper. Her gaze snapped to his face and her heart leapt in joyous response.

She smothered it. "Your Highness, you mustn't talk, and you mustn't try to move."

His gray eyes remained intent. "Where are we? Elysium?"

She dismissed the romantic imagery. "We're in a cove up the coast from the sage's seminary. You washed ashore here. Your ship sank in a storm the night before last. Do you remember?"

He nodded. His studious gaze unnerved her.

She averted her eyes. "I have some water here, but it's not much. I'll leave it with you and go for help."

Lightning-quick he caught her wrist, his grip surprisingly strong. "Don't leave me, Malena."

The pet name, one that only her parents used, caused her heart to stutter in her chest. She jerked her hand from his weakening grasp. He only grimaced and shifted his shoulders against the sand.

"You mustn't try to move, your Highness." His request that she remain made her second-guess her proper course of action. She set the flask beside him and stripped the cloak from her shoulders, bunching it to prop beneath his head. He groaned as she elevated him those few inches, but the first swig of water brought immediate relief.

Silence spread across the foggy cove. She looked again to the ocean, anxious for signs of that mysterious creature. The fog shifted against the waves, but nothing emerged from its depths. She offered the prince another sip, her ears ever alert for approaching sounds. Her group was miles away by now, or she would have yelled for help.

When half the flask was gone, her patient blinked, and his gaze grew more alert. Magdalena returned to rummaging through her bag. At the bottom, half bruised from the jostling of a dozen packets and vials, was a plum someone had handed her for breakfast when she had left the seminary doors. She'd had no appetite, thankfully. In a deft movement she cut a narrow slice and wedged it between her patient's dry, parted lips.

The prince, whose searching eyes observed the fog above, inhaled sharply and coughed. He reached trembling fingers toward his mouth, but she stayed his hand.

"You're dehydrated," Magdalena said. "The water and this are the best I can do. I'll cut up the rest and you can work on it while I get some help—"

"Don't leave me," he said again. He shifted the sliver of plum in his mouth to talk around it. Every phrase he spoke was a labor. "Give me a minute. I'll come with you."

She couldn't stop the disbelief that cut from her throat. "Your Highness, you're not leaving this cove on your own two feet." The only path in or out was the rock-strewn trail by which she had come, a trail that only manifest when the tide went out, and that would require far too much effort for someone in the prince's condition to navigate. She glanced anxiously that direction. The sooner she went for help, the better. Her initial, overwhelming gratitude at this miracle of finding him alive had faded in the reality before her: she could not transport him from this place on her own. She would collapse beneath his broad-shouldered physique if she tried.

She would have to leave him, trusting that he would remain safe in the sheltered cove, that no chittering deep-sea creatures would prey upon him in her absence.

Anxiously she scanned the lapping waters again for any sign of bulbous eyes. Nothing but foam-crested waves met her gaze. She cut another sliver of plum and fed it to the prince.

"I have to leave you here and go for help," she said.

He chewed the slice, watching her with half-lidded eyes. "You have to?"

"You need more treatment than what I have with me, your Highness."

"I have a name, Malena."

Her brows shot up, and so did the defensive wall around her heart. She might have attributed his words to delirium or shock, but he was more alert now—alert enough that she wondered at his resilience.

Her voice turned curiously detached. "Does everyone at court address the crown prince by his name?"

He wheezed a feeble scoff and rolled his head on her cloak, his eyes focusing further up the cove. "If my father gave an award for the longest-held grudge, you'd win it no contest."

She'd never heard such cynicism from him. The prince was charming to a fault, not cynical. Still, she tightened her resolve. "There's no grudge. I'm only following the rule."

He pinned her with a stare. "The rule, Magdalena, was that I couldn't show favor to one person over another. You and I are the only ones here, so I'm not favoring you over anyone else."

The spark in his eyes soothed her worries over his health. She sliced the plum again, a larger piece, and tucked it between his lips. "So if there were others with me, you would ask them to call you by your name as well?"

Exasperation crossed his face. He struggled to sit up, but she pushed his shoulder to the ground, for the moment stronger than him.

"I am dying," he said around pieces of half-chewed fruit. "Is this how you treat a dying man?"

But he wasn't dying, and they both knew it.

She glanced wistfully in the direction that she had come. "If I don't tell someone soon that I've found you and you really do die, your father will have me arrested and thrown in his dungeons."

"If you leave me here alone, *I* will have you arrested and thrown in his dungeons."

"You need treatment, your Highness."

"Just use your magic to heal me."

"That's not how my magic works. You know it's not. Or—" Her face flooded with embarrassment, for why should he know any such thing? Most people's magic worked that way, so naturally he would assume hers did too. Quietly she rephrased her statement. "It's not how it works. I can't heal you."

"No. You can only feel what's wrong with me."

Her breath caught in her throat as she met his studious gaze. He remembered. "That's right," she murmured.

"So what is wrong with me, Magdalena?"

She pursed her lips and listed the symptoms she had sensed. "Which is why," she finished, "I should be finding someone to help you."

"No. You should stay here and feed me more of your cloying plum. Help will find us."

She shook her head in frustration. "No one but me knows you're here. No one is going to come."

"They'll come looking for you when you don't turn up. Won't they?"

The way he asked her, as though questioning whether anyone would even miss her at the seminary, made her question it as well. Master Demsley had known what a state her mind was in. He might leave her to her own devices for the whole day. The fog steadily dissipated, and the muted disk of a sun behind it would burn hot as it climbed higher in the sky. She would need to shelter the prince. The vibrant color on his forehead, on his arms and at his throat, testified of his prolonged exposure already.

His voice stirred her from her observation. "You worry too much. More plum, Magdalena."

"I thought you said it was cloying." But she cut another sliver and placed it in his waiting mouth.

He chewed, thoughtful. "In truth, it's the best thing I've ever tasted. Better still because it comes from your hand."

Her expression turned instantly sour, and he huffed a laugh. Though it was at her expense, she was glad to see the humor return to his face.

"You haven't changed at all," he said.

Regret snaked through her. "Neither have you."

"And why should I? Everyone's always told me I'm perfect."

She cut the next piece a bit too viciously. He wasn't ready for it, but she pushed it between his teeth anyway. Mentally she resolved to ignore whatever else he might say.

But, as was his nature, he prodded at her.

"Court is so dull without you. Why did you never return?"

She spared him an incredulous look, her quickest defense against a rising blush. "I'm bound to the sage's seminary."

"But surely you have holidays. Breaks. Weekends. You can't be in classes every single day of the year."

"What few I have I use to visit my parents."

He grunted and looked away. "If I didn't know any better I'd say you didn't like me."

Magdalena's scowl deepened. "Don't sulk, your Highness. You know that everyone loves you."

One brow arched. "Including you?"

Her mouth thinned. If he remembered her, he already knew the answer to that question. "I said everyone, didn't I?" She chipped another slice of plum from its stone and held it toward him.

The prince took it from her. His eyes danced with mischief. "I used to get out of so many awful outings thanks to you."

"I know. And everyone always blamed me for spoiling things."

"I'm glad my little contrarian hasn't changed, but I do wish you would find the time to visit me instead of your parents. Even once or twice a year would have staved off my boredom."

Magdalena burrowed deeper into her cynicism. "If I were anyone else I might mistake your flirtation for something more serious, Highness."

"If you were anyone else I wouldn't flirt," he replied.

Her heart flip-flopped in her chest. The firm conviction that he didn't mean anything—that he was only *staving off his boredom*—kept her senses in check. "You're too bold, especially for a crown prince."

He rolled up onto one elbow, the better to pin her with a stare. "And why shouldn't I be? I just almost died."

Magdalena prodded at his shoulder, but he was stronger now and resisted her. "Yes, and everyone thinks that you are dead. I should be looking for someone to help you instead of sitting in the sand feeding you bits of plum."

"You're helping me. Lend me your lap, would you?"

Before she could even think to protest, he flopped his head onto her folded legs, his cheek upon her thigh as though she were a convenient pillow instead of a human.

"*Your Highness*," she hissed, her blush renewing tenfold. "I've already given you my cloak to lay your head on."

But he closed his eyes as though asleep, and all he said was, "I have a name, Magdalena."

Mortification crashed upon her like the waves against the shore. She swallowed the knot that worked up her throat, tempering her embarrassment behind indignation. "You have my cloak, Prince Finnian."

He only settled against her with a sigh. Sleep reclaimed him all too readily, and Magdalena, well aware of how near his brush with death had been, resigned herself to playing the role of furniture for an hour.

Chapter Two

THE SEMINARY HALLS BUZZED with excitement. Magdalena would sooner have retreated to her room than tread the gauntlet of gawking girls, but Master Demsley kept a firm hand upon her arm, under strict orders from the prince not to let her run off. Finnian, weak as a kitten, lounged upon a stretcher carried by the school's gardener and Master Demsley's personal assistant, Simon. He kept his eyes shut and his limbs loose for dramatic effect, posing a picture of tragic, iconic heroism. The image spoiled only when he would crack open one eye to check that Magdalena had not bolted.

Master Demsley himself had come looking for her by sea, with Simon to row the dory. Their astonishment at discovering her companion had fueled a rather hasty journey back. The only hiccup came in Finnian's reluctance to board a boat of any type, but his objections dissolved when Magdalena hopped in and offered to row the dory home while the pair of men carried the prince over the narrow ridge. Master Demsley watched the exchange with a shrewd eye. His assistant, less subtle, openly gaped.

"If this thing capsizes, I'll have you flogged," the prince told Magdalena when he curled up on the flat bottom of the vessel.

"It won't capsize," she said. The fog had cleared to reveal a blue sky with fluffy white clouds strewn across its expanse. Even the wind only waffled the water, barely more than a breeze.

Relief at their rescue had loosened the knot of anxiety in her chest. Had the day waxed much hotter, it would have forced her back to the seminary on her own, with worry for the prince's safety in her absence and whether she could convince anyone that he had truly washed ashore.

Master Demsley peppered her with questions as he tended his royal charge on the journey. Finnian endured the transfer of responsibility without a word until the dory ran aground. Magdalena, all too eager to escape his presence, had already climbed halfway out when he ordered her to stay. Master Demsley sent Simon ahead for help while everyone else remained with the boat.

"You don't need me anymore," Magdalena had whispered to the lounging prince, but he ignored her.

By the time Simon returned, having dispatched a messenger to the palace and retrieved the gardener and a stretcher, faces lined the windows of the seminary perched on the cliffs above. The braver girls ventured out into the yard, and a squeal of recognition from their midst sent the whole company aflutter.

"*A miracle!*"

"He's alive! He's alive!"

The rush of excitement pulsed against Magdalena's senses until she wanted to retch. The girls' joy turned to envy as their attention shifted past the prince to the tiny entourage that attended him, and to her in particular.

"If her magic told her he was alive, she should have let us know instead of hogging the news."

That wasn't how her magic worked, and as magicians themselves they all knew it. Logic and reason had fled their ranks, however.

Master Demsley gave his own chambers, the finest in the seminary, to the prince and set the gardener to watch the door against any enterprising visitors. He and Simon administered fluids and salves while Magdalena edged closer to the exit.

"Where do you think you're going?" Finnian called.

An exasperated huff left her lips. "You *don't* need me here, your Highness."

"I'll tell you when I don't need you."

"Wouldn't you rather I was gone?"

"Why? You've already seen me at my worst. Maybe you can come give me a shave."

Her expression flattened. "I'd hate for my hand to slip and cut your throat."

The prince's brows shot up. Master Demsley and his assistant both turned such shocked looks upon her that she blushed a vibrant hue, but she didn't retract the statement.

"Simon will give you a shave if you wish it, your Highness," said the schoolmaster with all decorum.

"I rather think I do," Finnian said, his voice stiff. As the assistant scurried to retrieve the needed supplies, the prince leveled a crusty glare at Magdalena. "It's a capital offense, threatening to harm my noble person."

"I said I *didn't* want to cut your throat," she replied. "My hands aren't steady right now."

He grunted, a furrow between his brows.

"Have you eaten anything today, Magdalena?" Master Demsley asked in a casual tone, seemingly intent upon applying salve to his patient's sunburn.

The prince's frown deepened. She averted her gaze as her blush heightened. "No."

Silence filled the room, smothering her until Finnian broke it. "Why haven't you eaten?"

Magdalena glanced sullenly to the door, her denied escape. Master Demsley answered for her.

"Because she fed the only breakfast she took with her this morning to you, your Highness." He finished his application and surveyed his glistening work with a nod. "Shall I have refreshment brought up? It will be plain fare, I'm afraid, until we're certain your stomach can handle more."

"Yes," said the prince, "and bring enough for her, too. I can't have a woman fainting on my account. Sit down, Malena. You're not going anywhere."

She scowled. Tempted though she was to remain standing out of spite, her harrowed night and stressful morning were catching up with her. If the prince truly meant to keep her in his sight—for whatever purpose he chose—she might as well sit.

"Not there," he said when she dropped into a chair on the far side of the room. "Bring it over here and sit by me."

A glance from her schoolmaster warned her to swallow the retort on her tongue. Obediently she dragged the chair across the room and set it by the prince's bedside, where she had a prime view when Simon returned and administered the requested shave.

Not that she watched.

Her hands jittered in her lap. Her emotions, kept so tightly wound within her, threatened to burst from their confines. She focused on the window and the tufts of clouds beyond its diamond panes. Movement encroached her periphery. The prince's hand groped the air as he held his head and neck steady under Simon's razor.

Magdalena intercepted the flailing appendage. "What are you doing?"

His grip tightened. He said not a word but kept her hand prisoner with his.

The shave was nearly complete when a hiss emitted from Simon's lips. Magdalena sat up straight, instinctively squeezing the prince's fingers. "What's wrong?"

"Bruises on his neck," said the assistant. "They look like—" His voice abruptly cut out. Red flooded his face to the tips of his ears.

"Like what?" the prince asked.

"Never mind," said Simon quickly. He resumed the shave, moving to block Magdalena as she craned her head to glimpse the mysterious injury.

Prince Finnian was no so easily fobbed off. "They look like *what*?"

"I spoke out of place, your Highness. Forgive me, please."

"Magdalena, what do they look like?"

Simon cast a self-conscious glance over his shoulder, but Magdalena had already seen the marks upon the patient's neck. A series of small, mottled purple circles twisted up his throat toward his ear. Her hold upon the prince's hand went slack as she contemplated exactly what he had been doing when the storm hit his ship. Before she could pull away, he tightened his grip.

Master Demsley, curious, wandered around from the other side of the bed. He readily supplied the answer no one else would give. "They look like love-marks, your Highness."

"*Excuse* me?"

"The mark made when blood vessels break under pressure from suction—"

"I know what a love-mark is," Finnian interrupted, his exasperation almost palpable. "Why are there any on my neck? Magdalena, just what were you doing while I slept on the beach?"

Her jaw dropped and she jerked her hand, but he had anticipated this reaction and held fast.

"I'm joking," he said over her indignant squeak. "But I've no more idea how I got those marks than you do."

"I can think of some possibilities," she said, still trying to wrest her hand from his determined grasp.

Master Demsley decided it best to intervene. "A number of sea creatures might cause such marks: octopuses have suction cups on their tentacles, and certain fish and eels attach themselves by a similar method. The bruising is at least a day or two old, and it was beneath the growth of facial hair. It's safe to assume it's a relic of your ocean ordeal, your Highness."

This glib explanation didn't clear the prince of the debauchery that such marks usually indicated. Instead, flimsy and implausible, it gave him an excuse that no one would question outright.

But Finnian replied in stiff tones, "We don't have to assume anything. We have an empath right here."

The weight of his words hit Magdalena like a fist to the gut. "I hardly think—" Her protest died in her throat as three pairs of eyes pinned her with open expectation. Her voice lowered to a mutter. "It's no one's business but your own where you got those marks, your Highness."

"Yes, and I would very much like to know."

By the mulish set of his jaw, she could see that he wouldn't permit her to refuse. Embarrassment rose upon her face. Grudgingly she closed her eyes and allowed her magical senses to expand.

Darkness, and flashes of light from the roiling ocean surface above. Slender limbs encircled the sinking body, while a face buried itself against the neck and—

Magdalena disconnected from the vision with a sharp inhale. Bulbous eyes and pointed teeth flashed before her.

"It was a sea creature." The words left her lips on a whisper. She didn't know what else to say, so chaotic was the imagery. Something had caught hold of the prince and given him those marks upon his neck. Whether it was the same chittering something that had lurked in the misty waters at the cove or whether her paranoid mind linked those two creatures together, she could not determine.

She met the prince's stare, his gray eyes intent upon her. He said nothing, but his expression spoke of vindication and—even more fiercely—of a desperate need for an ally. Magdalena ceased striving to free her hand. The schoolmaster's assistant completed the last few strokes of the shave as an awkward silence blanketed the room.

Simon glanced toward the clasped hands as he wiped the razor clean on a towel. He moved away to pack up the shaving kit.

Magdalena leaned close and whispered, not as waspishly as she might have intended, "You're turning me into a spectacle."

The prince maintained his steady gaze. "You're the only person here I know." The waver in his quiet voice betrayed the fear that lurked beneath his cocksure façade. Two nights ago a storm had ripped him into the briny ocean. He had passed more than a day in its clutches and washed ashore on the brink of death.

Her heart tightened in her chest. Instinctively she pressed his hand between both of hers.

Finnian looked up at the bed curtains. The small, satisfied smile on his lips left her to wonder if that moment of vulnerability had been sincere or manipulative—or a combination of both. She settled cynically back in her chair, but she maintained her hold upon his hand until his eyelids drooped and his grip went lax.

He dozed off and on throughout the afternoon. Toward dusk he woke with a gasp, sweat beading upon his forehead. Magdalena, who sat next to him with a book she only read when he was conscious, examined him.

"Are you in pain?" she asked. "Should I call Master Demsley?"

The prince peered at her face. His breath left his lungs in a sigh of relief. He reclaimed her hand from atop her book, his gaze unfocused. "My body keeps rocking up and down, as though the waves still churn around me, as though their clammy grip still cradles me close and chatters in my ears."

"Chatters?" she echoed with a shiver.

He only squeezed her hand again. "I'm glad you're flesh and blood, Malena."

Her defenses renewed under his familiar address. Quietly she asked, "Where did you hear that name, and why do you keep using it?"

The prince stilled. "Do you not like it?"

"Everyone calls me Magdalena."

"Your parents don't." She frowned, and he favored her with a wry smile. "You must know they visit court at least once a year—much better at paying homage to their allied king than you are. I've always asked them about you, and your father always slips and calls you Malena half a dozen times. I guess that's how I think of you now."

Her heart quickened in her chest despite her efforts to keep it at bay. "You ask my parents about me?"

"It's only polite," he said modestly. The disappointment

that shot through her shifted to chagrin when he added, "If you'd visit, I wouldn't have to ask them."

She pulled her hand from his and opened her book.

"Retreating into her own mind as usual," the prince murmured, seemingly careless.

A commotion in the hall drew their attention. The door flung open, and the gardener announced in quavering tones, "His Majesty King Ronan to see you, your Highness."

Magdalena scooted from her chair as quick as she could stand, her eyes huge upon the king of Corenden as he swept into the room. He took one look at the occupant of the bed and flung himself upon the young man in a crushing embrace.

"Father," Prince Finnian wheezed, patting his sire's back. As the hug persisted, he frowned over the king's shoulder to Magdalena. She edged toward the open doorway and the crowds that clustered beyond.

The king drew back, pawed at his son's face is disbelief, and hugged him again. "Finnian, Finnian—we thought you were dead."

"And I might have been if Magdalena hadn't found me."

She froze, mere inches from her escape. The king turned watery eyes upon her, and Magdalena dropped into an awkward curtsey.

"You have my thanks, young lady," King Ronan said.

Relief flooded through her: nowhere in his face was a hint of recognition. She ducked her head again, ignoring Finnian's suddenly critical glance upon her.

"Where's Mother?" the prince asked.

"At the palace. She took ill when news of your ship arrived, and I didn't want to get her hopes up until I'd seen you with my own eyes. Is he safe to travel, Master Demsley?"

"Yes, sire, he should be. He's in remarkable condition, all things considered."

"Then I will remove him to his home, where he belongs."

Finnian sat up on his elbows. "What, tonight? It's getting dark out."

"We'll travel quickly, my son," said his father. "I would not have your mother in grief any longer than necessary."

Across the room, Magdalena met the prince's gaze. She tipped her head in acknowledgement and slipped through the crush of bodies at the door as a scowl descended upon his face.

The rule was still very much in place. He would not favor her in front of his father, and that spoke volumes more than the hundred little flirtations he had made throughout the day. The prince was charming, but it was the same façade it had always been.

Her fellow students spared her sidelong glowers as she pressed through the throng, but so intent were they upon glimpsing the royals that they let her go. She broke free of the crowd and jogged through deserted halls to her own small bedroom, where she shut the door and leaned her back against it. Misery and relief clawed up her throat. She sank to the floor and buried her head in her arms.

The prince was alive. He would return to his world, and she would remain in hers, but he was alive, and that was all that mattered.

The tangled, knotted emotions within her burst in a torrent of tears. She was glad, and despairing, and exhausted all rolled into one. The onslaught lasted only a short while before she reined it in, but for the second night in a row, she skipped dinner and went straight to bed.

Chapter Three

WHEN CLASSES RESUMED the following morning, Magdalena stiffly took her place among her peers. She ignored the whispers behind her back and shut off her senses to any magical empathy. Injured feelings abounded among the schoolgirls, many of whom begrudged that the man they actively fantasized about had paid special favor to such a cold fish.

"I don't care if she knew him as a child. Why was she allowed to stay with him all day when none of us could get within ten yards of his door?"

When lunchtime came, she wisely skirted past the dining hall, intending to spend the hour in the solitude of her own room. She rounded the last corner and stopped short. Two soldiers guarded her door while another pair marched from within, carrying a trunk between them—her trunk, to be precise.

"What are you doing?" she asked, hurrying to intercept them.

One of the guards stepped in her path. "Hello, lovely." He drew the words out as though relishing every consonant. Magdalena, intent upon following her stolen goods, tried to sidestep, only for him to block her way.

"You are Magdalena of Ondile, I presume?"

Mention of her father's duchy snapped her attention from the fast retreating trunk. She looked up, stricken, into a handsome face. Blue eyes twinkled, and a smile curved up one side of his mouth. Taking her lack of response as an affirmative to his question, he raised one of her hands to his lips.

Magdalena snatched it away before he could complete the flirtatious gesture. "Who are you? Why are you taking my things?"

"Captain Gilroy Byrne at your service, milady. I come with orders from the royal court to retrieve you and your belongings."

Dread plunged through her. "If his Highness thinks this is—"

"Not his Highness. His Majesty."

She recoiled. "What?"

"I come on the king's orders," said the captain. "Between you and me, I rather suspect his Highness the crown prince would prefer that the likes of me never came within three leagues of you, if you catch my meaning."

He winked, and she scowled. "No, I don't catch your meaning at all."

His brows shot upward, but she was saved his rebuttal when her schoolmaster stepped from her door carrying her cloak and her healer's satchel.

"Ah, Magdalena," Master Demsley said, and he gestured vaguely to the pair of soldiers who yet remained. "You are to go to the palace, a great honor indeed."

"But—"

"The king has offered you an apprenticeship with his own healer, my dear," he said.

Her mouth opened and shut with nary a sound. No one could decline an apprenticeship at the palace, however unsought or unwanted it might be. Her thoughts roiled. As loath as she felt to reenter that glittering sphere, she would be little more than a servant—and thus somewhat sheltered from association with the royal family and court.

Still, "Must I leave today?" she asked in a small voice.

"This very hour," said the captain with a suave grin. "His Majesty was most specific. We'll have you home and installed in your new room by dinnertime."

Master Demsley pressed her cloak and bag into her hands. "It's for the best. Truly I wish you every happiness."

She couldn't stop the confusion that twisted up her face at this strange farewell. Nor did she get a chance to respond. Captain Byrne whisked her in the same direction that her trunk had disappeared, one casual arm draped upon her shoulders.

"I beg your pardon, but I can walk very well on my own," she said, a sliver of ice in her voice. She skirted out from beneath his touch.

He tutted. "No need to be so frigid. We have a long ride ahead together."

Magdalena halted in her tracks. Her expression hardened into something so obstinate that even this seeming ladies' man appeared momentarily fearful.

"I can walk very well on my own," she said again, enunciating every syllable to deadly effect.

He backed away, hands raised in surrender, and allowed her to proceed. She swept past him with all the dignity she could muster, her ears alert as his footsteps tapped along the hall behind her. Out in the seminary's courtyard, an open carriage awaited. Two of the guards had mounted their horses already. The third climbed onto the box to drive. Magdalena flung her cloak around her shoulders and ascended on her own power.

To her consternation, Captain Byrne climbed up as well and sat directly across from her. The carriage lurched forward. He regarded her with shrewd eyes. "You don't have time for the small fish now that you've set your sights on the prince, is that it?"

Still in the throes of her quiet wrath, she managed not to blush. "I beg your pardon?"

"No, nothing," he said, and he sat back.

She wasn't going to let him drop the subject so easily, though. "What's that supposed to mean, that I've set my sights on the prince? How does being forced from the sage's seminary into an apprenticeship portend that I've set my sights on anyone?"

His brows arched, but he couldn't maintain eye contact. He looked away with a puff-cheeked sigh. "Whooh. He has his work cut out for him with you," he muttered under his breath, the words barely discernible over the clip-clop of the horses' hooves.

"Who has?"

"The palace healer, of course," Captain Byrne replied, though the answer came too quick. Magdalena settled into her seat and drew a book from one of her deep pockets. She pretended to read for the whole drive, turning pages even though her eyes only glided over the words without seeing them. From her periphery she kept watch for any odd moves from the overly familiar captain, but he only tipped his hat over his face and slept. When he started to snore, she turned her thoughts to more troublesome men.

If Finnian had put his father up to this stunt, she was going to wring his neck, prince or no prince.

The further they traveled along the coastal highway, the tighter her windpipe constricted. All too soon, the palace of Corenden glittered against the shimmering ocean, perched where the land met the water. She fought against an onslaught of carefully suppressed memories—playtime in the garden, expeditions along the shore, gossiping and backbiting among the girls vying for the young prince's attention. Beneath the sparkling façade, a toxic atmosphere had flourished.

And now she returned as a glorified servant to the crown. Would that someone else had wandered to that sheltered cove instead of her.

(Except that a smothered part of her was glad that she had found him instead of anyone else. There was no real harm in worshipping the prince as long as she knew such worship would lead to nothing.)

The carriage clattered onto cobblestone streets, past docks lined with broad, tall-masted boats, until the palace loomed above, its towers bathed in the orange light of the setting sun. Captain Byrne roused and straightened as they passed onto the smooth pavers of the palace drive. He spared Magdalena a sidelong glance. She kept her nose in her book.

They stopped beside a shaded entrance—one of the doors designated for servants rather than the grand, sweeping staircase that dignitaries and guests ascended. Captain Byrne hopped to the ground and offered to help Magdalena. He showed no surprise when she declined. She filed in behind him to a dark hall as eerie nostalgia worked its way from her stomach to her nose. She knew the halls as well as she knew her own hands. Swallowing the lump of apprehension in her throat, she drew her cloak closer around her and focused on putting one foot in front of the other.

"The palace healer is tending to the crown prince tonight," said Captain Byrne. "The king instructed that you be brought to your quarters this evening, and that you remain there until Master Asturias can orient you tomorrow. Someone will bring you your supper. Is that satisfactory?"

She longed to say no, or to ask whether a contrary answer would make any difference. Instead of wasting her breath, she merely pursed her lips and arched an eyebrow.

The captain averted his gaze and kept walking. When they arrived at the tiny chamber—little more than a closet, really—

he stayed long enough to see his men wedge Magdalena's trunk between the bed and the wall, and then he slinked down the hall out of sight. The other soldiers tipped their caps and made similar escapes.

Magdalena shut the door and locked it. She flopped onto the bed with a heavy sigh. The tangled emotions exorcised the previous night had returned tenfold. The close room with its narrow window seemed a prison cell in the falling darkness.

Chapter Four

THE CRY OF A SEAGULL roused her half an hour before dawn. By the time a light knock tapped at her doorway, she was up, dressed, and resigned to her fate. She opened the portal not to a servant, but to a gaunt, olive-skinned elder, one whose face she recalled all too well. He peered down his hooked nose at her, haughty curiosity fixed upon him, with not a sliver of recognition.

Which was, perhaps, for the best.

"Master Asturias, I presume?" she said.

He tipped his nose a fraction higher into the air. "I should have you know that I do not favor apprentices. I particularly do not favor female apprentices. On the king's orders alone I have accepted you, but don't expect any special treatment."

Having completed this officious speech, he spun on his heel and walked away. Magdalena, assuming she was meant to follow, pulled her bag over head and shut the door behind her. She dogged his footsteps, her confusion growing the further into the palace they progressed. Master Asturias rattled off place names and instructions with vague gestures and little heed for whether she heard him.

"The kitchens are down that corridor. You eat with the other servants in the servants' hall next to it. You have an hour at dawn for breakfast. My infirmary is here. You're not to touch anything without my express permission. The passage up ahead leads to the state rooms, where the king meets with local and foreign dignitaries. You have no business there, so you're never to intrude. This wing houses quarters for visiting nobility. Again, you have no business there. The royal quarters are that direction, and they are completely forbidden. Do you understand?"

They had paused in a wide rotunda where three hallways intersected. The marble floors gleamed and sunlight filtered through colored windows above. Master Asturias glared down at her, waiting for her answer.

"I understand," Magdalena said. Perhaps the king should have thrown her in prison. Surely this was some sort of punishment.

"If so, then—" His voice strangled in his throat as he focused over her shoulder. Magdalena instinctively turned. The healer rudely shoved past her. "Your Highness, you should not be out of bed."

Her gaze connected with that of Prince Finnian, who, apparently, had been sneaking from his quarters. He stopped dead in his tracks, his eyes huge upon her.

Master Asturias, oblivious, approached the young royal as though to herd him back the way he had come. "Your father and mother both insist that you remain abed for another day, your Highness."

Finnian skirted around his outstretched hands. "What are you doing here?" he asked Magdalena, wonder and confusion warring upon his face.

Her feet seemed rooted into the tiles and her tongue weighed like lead in her mouth. So he really *hadn't* known anything of her coming.

He approached like a skittish horse, stopping several feet from her to observe her in puzzled silence—as though she were a mirage that might vanish from his sight. She fought to control her quickening pulse. He looked good. The high, starched collar of his shirt hid the sea creature's marks on his neck, and only his fading sunburn provided evidence of his recent ordeal.

The palace healer followed his recalcitrant patient. "Your Highness, this is my new apprentice. She—"

"Rubbish," said the prince, his gaze never leaving Magdalena's face.

Master Asturias bristled. "I beg your pardon?"

Finnian's voice pitched with exasperation as he confronted the healer. "She can't be your apprentice. That's practically a servant. Her father's the Grand Duke of Ondile, and she's his only child. What idiot proposed pulling the heir of one of our sovereign allies into servitude?"

A gurgle sounded from Master Asturias's throat.

"And you," Finnian cried, turning his attention on Magdalena. "What have you to say for yourself?"

She maintained her calm despite a jittery heartbeat. "I didn't have a choice. Soldiers showed up at the seminary yesterday, confiscated my things, and loaded me into a carriage."

"And you didn't pull rank on any of them?"

She shifted, unable to meet his gaze. "I don't… I mean…"

His familiar, twinkling charm crept onto his face in the form of a winsome smile. "You know, Malena, if you wanted to come see me so badly, you didn't have to go through such a charade."

Her temper snapped. "We don't use rank at the seminary. I'm out of the habit. And if I did want to see you—which I didn't—I would have come on my own power instead of having a smarmy captain practically frogmarch me here."

"Smarmy—?" Dismay twisted his mouth. "You mean Gil brought you?"

"Gil?" she echoed, coldly distant.

"Captain Byrne."

"That was the name."

To her surprise, Finnian raked one hand through his hair and paced the length of the rotunda. Silence prevailed as he processed this new revelation, until he arrived at a conclusion. "I'll go see my father. I'll have everything cleared up in an instant. Or were you coming to see him now?"

Magdalena spared a sidelong glance at the elder healer, who seemed to think silence was his best option. "Master Asturias was instructing me on the layout of the palace."

"Why? You used to live here."

"I didn't get the chance to tell him that."

Finnian barked a laugh. He snatched at her wrist to pull her along with him, but she evaded his grasp.

"Don't make me a spectacle here too, your Highness," she said in a low voice.

He paused. Something akin to hurt flashed through his eyes, but he shook it off. "Come with me, both of you."

Magdalena glanced longingly down the passage that led back to her tiny room, but disobedience to the crown prince was not an option. Glumly she fell in step behind him, Master Asturias stiff-backed beside her. She fixed her attention on the floor as they walked. The familiar patterned marble dredged up memories of laughing childhood games played along this very hall.

The prince stopped at the door to the king's private parlor, but only long enough to rap a sharp rhythm against it. He shoved through with a contrived smile plastered on his face. His jovial voice rang out into the hall. "Good morning, Father, Mother. Look who I just found."

Magdalena shared a perturbed glance with Master Asturias. They both filed into the room, where the king and queen ate their breakfast. King Ronan kept his expression aloof when he spied Magdalena. Queen Orla almost choked on her eggs.

"You've met Master Asturias and his new apprentice," said the king. His wife sputtered and coughed, but her maid scurried from the side of the room to pat her back, so he focused his attention on his son. "I'm sure one or both of them told you to return to your bed for the day."

"Yes, Master Asturias did." Prince Finnian beamed at his sire.

The queen buried her face in her napkin, her cheeks almost purple as she expelled the errant food particles from her trachea.

"And yet here you are, not in your bedchamber at all." The king's voice held a reproving edge.

The prince ignored it. "I'll get back there eventually. Magdalena says that Gil brought her here yesterday, and if Gil was involved, that means it was on your orders."

His father adopted a false façade that matched the son's almost perfectly. "An apprenticeship to the palace healer is a great honor. What better, more appropriate reward could we offer the young woman who performed such a marvelous service on the crown's behalf?"

The queen drowned her coughing fit in a glass of water, her stricken face drawn tight.

"I can think of several," said the prince. His expression turned studious. "I'm more curious, though: how does the Grand Duke of Ondile feel about you apprenticing out his daughter as though she were a common peasant?"

King Ronan froze. His gaze slid to Magdalena, confirmation that not only had he not recognized her on the night he retrieved his son from the seminary, but that her name had triggered no recognition until this very moment. The blood drained from his face.

His wife, meanwhile, recovered her wits and scooted from her chair. She circled around the table to envelop Magdalena in a perfume-laden hug. "How lovely to see you again, my dear.

It's been quite a few years since you've graced our courts with your beauty." She gushed over her gratitude for the help Magdalena had provided her son and launched into a speech about the terrifying two days she spent believing her child had met his death at sea.

None of this was enough to distract Magdalena from a very different, very quiet conversation taking place across the room.

The king leaned close to the prince and whispered, "You never said the girl who saved you was the Grand Duke's daughter."

Finnian replied in much the same tones. "I *told* you it was Magdalena of Ondile."

"There are probably dozens—*hundreds*—of Magdalenas in Ondile! How was I supposed to know—"

"You saw her with your own eyes! She used to live here, Father, until you and Mother sent her away."

"But you should have *said*—"

A frustrated growl erupted from Prince Finnian. The sound, so unlike him, caught his mother's attention. She arrested her story to ask, "Are you tired, dear? This is why we wanted you to stay in bed for another day or two."

"I'm not tired," Finnian snapped. He noticed Magdalena, as though he had briefly forgotten her presence, and schooled away his ire. "I merely wanted to learn how this interesting arrangement had come about. Now, *I'm* going to complete the tour Master Asturias was giving his new apprentice, and *you three* can stay here to work out the details of her service."

"Finnian—" his father began.

"It's the least we can do for such a distinguished guest," the prince said. He was already tucking Magdalena's arm against his side, guiding her to the door. A warning glance from him told her to go along with this.

The rule was to be set aside for the moment, it seemed. "So nice to see you again," Magdalena said as he led her away. She ducked her head, the closest she could get to a curtsey while moving so quickly.

Finnian pulled the door shut behind them. "What can I say?" The sincerity behind this question spoke an apology he had yet to voice.

And Magdalena did not want him to voice it. "Why should you say anything?" She attempted to extract her arm, but he held tight.

"I insist, Malena. I'll finish your tour while they get everything sorted for you."

Her heart sank, but she ruthlessly smothered the emotions that swelled. "Sorted for me how? If the king and queen send me home, there's no need to finish a tour."

He stared. "You consider the seminary your home?"

Confusion pulled through her. "No. Ondile is my home."

"But at most you'll return to the sage's seminary."

She couldn't stop the bitter laugh that bubbled up. "In disgrace? By now everyone there knows I was called here for an apprenticeship. Apprentices don't return unless they fail and require discipline. At this point, I'm bound for Ondile."

The quiet dismay upon his face upended her thoughts. She shifted her attention further up the hall. "It's all right. The seminary couldn't have kept me much longer. My brand of magic makes me more of a curiosity than a useful contributor, and it's rare enough that Master Demsley has exhausted all his resources on it already."

"I don't—" Finnian began. She glanced a question at him. He tried again. "Ondile is too far away. It's half a week or more to get there. I never intended to send you—"

"It's all right," she said again. His distress was spiking sharply enough that it seeped into her.

But her attempt to soothe fell short of its mark. "It's *not* all right." Finnian dropped her arm and stepped away from her. A wild look chased across his face. He glanced up the hall they had come, to the door behind which his parents discussed this situation with their palace healer. His mouth flattened. "Wait here."

He strode back that direction and disappeared into the room without so much as knocking. The door clicked shut, leaving Magdalena standing alone in a hall that was generally out of bounds for any but the royal family.

A fleeting urge to bolt coursed through her. How soon might she have before someone passed at either end of the corridor and saw her here, before they called guards to escort her off the premises? Her anxiety multiplied with each passing second, so that when the door opened and Finnian reappeared, relief swamped her in an instant. She moved instinctively closer. He tucked her arm against his side again.

"It's settled. Let's continue your tour, then."

"What's settled?" Magdalena asked.

"You're to remain as Master Asturias's apprentice," he said. "My father will write your father and explain everything. You won't return to your seminary in disgrace, or have to make the long trip to Ondile. Master Asturias is interested in working with an empath, too, so you can be of use to him. All that's left is to move you into proper quarters in the nobles' wing."

Her alarm spiked anew. "No!"

The prince frowned at her, suddenly uncertain. "No? I thought maybe you didn't mind the apprenticeship—"

"I don't. I mind quarters in the nobles' wing."

He stopped and turned his full bewilderment upon her.

At this point, she had nothing to lose by being frank. "Living among those girls was a nightmare, your Highness. The catty remarks, and the backbiting. Some of them were downright mean, and they were only children. I can't imagine what age has done to them."

His mouth rounded. "Oh. Well, the crowd's thinned from the old days. I think that most of the mean ones have gone back to their parents by now."

The mean girls were also the absolute least likely to vacate. She frowned as she considered this. "How could that possibly be?"

Finnian smiled his charming smile and patted her arm. "Easy as pie. I showed them special favor and my father sent them away." He laughed at his rule-breaking. Magdalena, meanwhile, considered the calculating nature this remark revealed.

"Like you're showing me special favor right now?" she asked. What game was he playing? With Finnian, there was always some ulterior motive lurking beneath his cheerful veneer.

But he only laughed again. "Don't worry. This is outside the rule. Here's the garden, just as it always was."

They crossed from shadowed hallway to brilliant sunlight, where flowers and trees basked and insects flittered through the air. The heady floral scents washed over Magdalena, invoking sweet nostalgia. She had loved to sprawl out upon the grass and read, once upon a time.

Impulsively she broke away from the prince to smell a cluster of pink blossoms. He chuckled behind her back. When she glanced at him in confusion, he said, "That's the first time you've smiled in six years."

Magdalena straightened, prim in her self-consciousness. "Don't be silly. Of course it's not."

He shrugged. "I haven't seen any of the others, so they don't count."

Her brows drew together in a decided frown, which only elicited another laugh from him.

"The world doesn't revolve around you, your Highness."

"Of course it doesn't. But what meaning has sunshine at night, even if it does exist?" Before she could respond, he turned wistful eyes upon the expanse of gardens. "I'd say you have about an hour before any of our noble residents stirs from their bedchambers, if you want to play out here."

"I'm a bit too old for playing," said Magdalena.

He favored her with a wry smile. "Are you? That's a shame. Come have some breakfast with me, then." He extended his hand toward her.

She wanted to take it, but a series of painful memories assaulted her. "Wouldn't that be breaking the rule?"

"I told you we're outside of the rule. Would you feel better if I sent word inviting everyone else to join us?"

Her reproving glare was answer enough. He laughed, and she accepted his hand, and together they passed back into the palace.

"Good morning," said a cheerful voice. Magdalena and the prince both dropped their hands behind their back, like guilty children caught in mischief. Captain Byrne smiled. "As long as you're out of your rooms today, your Highness, your father has asked that I watch over you."

Annoyance flashed across Finnian's face. He started to say something but swallowed it in favor of walking. Magdalena followed, and Captain Byrne fell in step beside her.

"So I hear you're not *a* Magdalena of Ondile, but *the* Magdalena of Ondile. My apologies for failing to recognize you."

She glanced up at the handsome captain but returned her gaze forward when their eyes met.

He chuckled. "You don't remember me, do you."

Finnian's shoulders stiffened in front of her. Magdalena, startled by the bald assertion, chose the easiest response.

"No, I don't."

There had been no Gil and certainly no Captain Byrne, to her recollection, in those bygone days.

The prince paused, glancing back. "You don't remember him because he's only been here for three years."

Magdalena frowned up at the captain, who only laughed again.

"You'd be surprised how many people claim they do remember me, though, milady." He winked.

With a warning glare to the flirtatious officer, Finnian drew Magdalena to walk beside him. They continued on their path, Captain Byrne in their wake.

Chapter Five

*M*AGDALENA'S RETURN to the palace of Corenden, along with her heroic role in rescuing the castaway prince, spread like wildfire. By day's end, hundreds of servants had peeked at her, and dozens of nobles had stopped by Master Asturias's infirmary on false pretenses.

The palace healer grew increasingly annoyed at the interruptions to his work. Magdalena intercepted the visitors and tended to their minor complaints in his stead.

"The palace might want to consider refinishing its furniture, what with the alarming number of splinters we've seen today," she said as the pink light of sunset stained the room.

Master Asturias only grunted from the corner where he mixed his healing elixirs.

It wasn't all the furniture that needed refinishing, of course. By now she could clearly see the worn settee where the ladies of the court had run their fingers—some of them repeatedly—to pick up their flimsy excuse to seek out this upstart girl who had returned to their ranks. They had spoken to her with honeyed words as she tended to them, oblivious that she could sense not only the nature of their injury but also its source.

When she brought out tweezers and a bandage, each girl had exhibited surprise. To a one they asked, "You can't heal it? I thought you had magic."

"That's not the type of magic I have," Magdalena always replied, her voice patient as she stooped close to extract the flecks of wood.

Master Asturias, who was a healing magician, remained in his corner. Each girl left the infirmary with hand salved and bandaged and presumably returned to her room without communicating anything of importance to her peers, as the next would appear armed with the same ignorance.

"There's a paste you can apply to slivers to swell them out of the skin," Master Asturias had commented after the third such encounter.

"I know," said Magdalena as she cleaned the sharp tweezers. Her fingers itched with pinpricks of phantom wounds up and down their lengths.

The healer had arched his brows but didn't interfere after that. It was, perhaps, petty of her to choose the more painful method for dealing with these visitors, but she had no incentive to offer them an easy fix for a frivolous malady they had caused themselves. Besides, the process hurt her as much as it hurt them.

Their final visitor came as the pink sunset bled into a twilit purple. Prince Finnian knocked on the door casing, with

Captain Byrne directly behind him. Master Asturias almost leapt from his workbench, his spindly fingers scrabbling for a vial he had set aside. A glance toward Magdalena told her that he would handle this patient, so she remained primly in her own corner of the room.

The palace healer whispered instructions to the prince as he gave him the vial. Finnian nodded, but he shifted his attention past the man to Magdalena. "Are you done for the day?"

"She's done," Master Asturias replied before Magdalena could say a word.

The prince accepted this answer as though she had spoken it with her own lips. "Will you walk with me, then?"

"Do you walk with all the ladies of the court one by one?" she asked.

He tipped his head toward the door. "Gil is here too. Come on."

Her master had already given her permission to go, and she'd be a fool to deny an invitation from the crown prince. Carefully she fell in step beside him. "Where do we walk?"

"To the ocean stairs."

The palace, perched as it was where the sea met the land, featured a staircase that descended directly into the waters. Low tide more fully revealed its marbled length, though the very bottom always remained submerged beneath the foaming waves. It served as relic of a storied past, when Corenden held alliance with the fay of the sea and the air—or so the palace folklore said. The stairs, positioned at the edge of a sheltered pavilion, provided an unhampered panoramic view of the horizon where the sea met the sky. Each night, when twilight seeped into shadow, the stars and the glittering waters sparkled like diamonds against the inky darkness.

"That's a rather romantic choice," Gil quipped from behind.

Magdalena and Finnian both turned an arch look upon him.

"Three's a crowd," Finnian said.

"Yes, which is why I thought it odd you would take both of us there." The captain favored him with a wry smile and earned a flat glower in return. The prince returned his attention to his requested walking companion.

"My father dispatched a letter to yours this morning. Will your parents be very upset that you're here as an apprentice?"

"Hardly," said Magdalena. Had she been apprenticed elsewhere, they would be incensed, but they would probably dance with joy to learn she had returned to the shimmering palace of Corenden. Their dismay back when her magic solidified still burned strong upon her memory.

As an only child of the Grand Duke she had one purpose in life: to marry well and thereby secure her ancestral duchy's continued prosperity. Her parents, affectionate though they were, sacrificed her childhood to that end. This present sojourn would likely rekindle the hopes that had died when she left court life for the sage's seminary.

"I would be glad if they receive the news well," Finnian said.

She spared him a skeptical glance and remained silent.

They passed along an open corridor where light and laughter filtered from balconies above. Music drifted down to them. The evening parties at the palace had been mesmerizing, glittering affairs in her youth: women in beautiful gowns and men in handsome suits moving in clusters and dancing together into the night. The children had attended until supper, after which the servants herded them off to bed—not that any of them had stayed there. They had watched from higher in the palace, from the tower balconies that afforded a bird's view of the whirling dancers below.

"Shouldn't you be up there with everyone?" she asked.

"I'm still recovering."

Behind them, Captain Byrne failed to contain a scoff.

"I beg your pardon, your Highness," he said when Finnian glared.

Magdalena redirected the conversation. "What still ails you?"

"I can't sleep." He raised the vial that Master Asturias had given him, studying its liquid contents against the far-off lights as he walked. "This is a sedative, if I dare take it."

"Why wouldn't you?"

"Can your magic show you a person's nightmares?"

She might have brushed this question off with a negligent wave, as she usually did when someone asked her about the nature of her abilities, but he peered at her with such intent eyes that a chill swept up her spine.

"No," she whispered. "I'm sorry."

"I'm glad. I'd rather not share them."

They arrived at the sheltered, shadowed pavilion, where the sea air breezed through marble balustrades that overlooked the cliffs. The ocean stairs descended in a steep, straight line against the precipice, and the waves crashed into them below.

The prince crossed the room and settled on the top step. Magdalena, after a moment's hesitation, joined him, and Captain Byrne did the same, on her other side.

"Nice night," the officer said, grinning.

It was. Stars patterned across the sky, except on the far horizon where dark clouds obscured them from sight. The breeze blew salt and something more upon it—a fresh, nighttime scent one could only find at the shore.

Finnian broke the tranquility. "I should have died out there."

"Oh, don't be morbid," said Gil. "Fate brought you back to us."

"It wasn't fate. It was something else."

Magdalena looked sharply to him. He briefly met her gaze but turned his own to the sedative in his hands. He twisted the vial between his fingers, its cut edges reflecting the dull light around them.

"Something dragged me downward when I fell into the water," said the prince. "It wrapped around me and dragged me down. And then it changed its mind, I suppose. The next thing I remember was the glare of the noonday sun and the ocean heaving around me. And that something still gripped me beneath the waves."

Her breath caught in her throat. "What was it? Did you see it?"

"No. I was in and out of consciousness. It stayed beneath the waves, but I knew it held me tight. Every so often…" He hesitated. "Every so often it would surface above my head, out of sight, and chatter something in my ear."

Magdalena sat up straight. The instinctive reaction drew both men's attention.

"What is it?" Finnian asked.

She shrank back. "No. It was…" She shook her head to clear it. Having told no one of the creature at the cove, now so many days removed from the incident, she questioned whether she had imagined it.

He caught her hand. "Malena, what is it?"

She spared a self-conscious glance at the captain on her other side. "There was…" She breathed deep and plunged ahead. "There was something in the water that morning when I found you. But I couldn't see it clearly through the fog."

"What did you see?"

She gathered her thoughts. The tale made her sound crazy, but if the prince had already encountered the creature, her added details might bring him peace of mind. "Eyes like marbles in a sleek, silver head. It had no nose, but its mouth was parted, with long, sharp teeth—"

"—and webbing between its fingers, and scales instead of skin," he interrupted. "It haunts my dreams, as though it's still out there watching, waiting."

"This is the most ghastly, unromantic conversation I've ever heard," Captain Byrne said. "If I have to chaperone you two, at least give me something worth my while to report."

Magdalena looked to him and then quizzically to the prince.

"Gil acts as chaperone so that I'm never alone with any of the ladies of the court," said Finnian, propping his elbow against his knee and his chin atop his palm. "It's part of the rules."

Rules, plural. Meaning they had multiplied, and that she was subject to them once again.

"I see. So you bring him along whenever you walk alone with one of us? Was it my night, or did I accidentally cut in line? Is this where you always come?"

"Don't be like that, Malena."

But she was already stiff-backed, the former intimate mood broken. "Well, I wouldn't want to break the rules."

"Oh, but you're a special case, milady," said Captain Byrne from her other side.

Finnian leaned forward with menace on his face. "A certain smug officer is about to get pitched down the stairs if he doesn't keep his mouth shut."

"Why would I be a special case?" Magdalena asked, unwilling to let this detail slide.

"None of the other ladies is apprenticed," the captain said, too glib for it to be the truth. He and the prince remained locked in a battle of wills, their eyes fixed upon one another.

She stood, disrupting the contest.

"What—?" said Finnian.

"As an apprentice, I should retire to my bed. I have to be up early tomorrow. Good night, your Highness. Captain."

The prince scrambled from the steps. "I'll walk you back."

She was already halfway to the exit. "Not necessary. I know my way around."

He let her go, remaining behind as an inky silhouette against the night sky.

Logic told her to be grateful, but disappointment and despair ate through it.

Chapter Six

Prince Finnian brought fresh flowers from the garden the next morning. He offered the bouquet to Magdalena in the infirmary, under the watchful eyes of Master Asturias and Captain Byrne.

She had battled her tumultuous feelings through the night, resolving to contain them regardless of what flirtations he might attempt. Accordingly, she plastered on a fake smile as she accepted the colorful bunch. "How lovely. Are you bringing flowers to all the ladies of the court today?"

"Actually, I am." He leaned in close and whispered with a wink, "But yours are the prettiest."

She frowned to hide the blush his tease invoked. A note of sarcasm tempered her obligatory gratitude. "Thank you, your Highness. I am honored."

He laughed and left her to her day's work. She stowed the small bouquet in an extra distillation flask. The flowers brightened her morning, but she would have sooner died than admit it to anyone—and to Finnian in particular.

At lunchtime, as she headed to the servants' hall to take her meal, he intercepted her.

"You're not actually a servant, you know." He tucked her arm in his and drew her in a different direction.

She glanced down the passageway for any sign of Captain Byrne. "Where's your shadow?"

"I slipped away while he wasn't looking. We're having lunch at the ocean stairs today."

"We?" Foreboding welled within her.

He smiled. "The younger nobles. The pavilion is a perfect gathering place on a day like this."

Magdalena dug in her heels. "I don't want to eat with the court nobles. I'm here as an apprentice, not as a guest."

He lowered his voice. "Everyone knows you're here. It would be strange if you didn't socialize."

"I'm not dressed for court."

The prince glanced her over. "What's wrong with what you're wearing?"

Her clothing, though of fine make, better suited her position in the infirmary than a luncheon with the noble class. The somber gray material would present a striking foil to the pastel silks and satins that most of the ladies at court favored.

"Are you joking?" she asked.

But not a hint of guile crossed his face. "You always look nice. Come on, Malena. It's officially my first day out of bed after my terrible ordeal, and lunch wouldn't be complete without you there."

"You were out of bed yesterday."

"Yes, but I wasn't supposed to be."

From down the hall, a shout interrupted this tête-à-tête. "Your Highness!" Captain Byrne, breathless, barreled at them. The prince stepped back a pace, though he spared Magdalena a wry sidelong glance. The captain joined them, his hands on his hips and a scowl on his face. "It's my job on the line if I lose sight of you, you know."

A charming smile broke across Prince Finnian's face. "What a perfect shame it would be to lose you."

Captain Byrne glowered. He shifted his irritated gaze to Magdalena.

"We met by chance on the way to the ocean stairs," said Finnian, with a glance that encouraged her to go along with the lie. She wisely kept her mouth shut.

"You know the rules, your Highness," said the captain. He pushed past the pair to lead the way.

Magdalena, tempted to protest her attendance, swallowed the words when Finnian tucked her arm in his again. Did he intend to walk with her into the pavilion like that? In front of all the court nobles?

Her curiosity got the best of her. She remained at his side, counting steps to keep herself calm. Surely he would drop her arm when they neared the threshold. They couldn't arrive together like... like...

He laid his other hand over her wrist and gave it an encouraging pat. The threshold loomed before them, with the buzz of conversation and light music.

"You're going to start rumors," Captain Byrne said over his shoulder.

"You mean they haven't started already?" Prince Finnian replied with a smile.

"Am I to be a spectacle?" Magdalena asked him under her breath. Anxiety blossomed within her.

The charming façade dropped as he looked to her with genuine concern. When he spoke, he did so as one who chose his words carefully. "You saved my life. You hold a place of honor here that no one can dispute."

They crossed the threshold. Conversations died as dozens of people shifted their attention to the pair.

Finnian's smile returned full force. "Hello, everyone. I've brought my little savior with me today." He squeezed Magdalena's hand and released her, crossing to greet the nearest cluster of guests. Others quickly moved to the space at her side, expressing their delight in seeing her and how grateful they were for the prince's safety.

"How lucky you were to find him," said one young lady in pale pink. "Everyone burst with joy when the king brought him home."

"Such a good thing you happened upon him," said her companion in spring green.

Mentions of luck and happenstance abounded in comment after comment. "It could have been anyone," they each seemed to say. "His favor toward you now is thanks to a fluke."

And they all spoke with such saccharine sincerity that Magdalena's head throbbed before even half an hour had passed. She already knew not to take Finnian's favor as genuine, but this receiving line of well-dressed, well-spoken peers drummed that mantra into her. She managed to swallow half a sandwich from the buffet against the wall, and with that token lunch consumed, made her exit.

"Rough crowd."

She jumped and clapped a hand to her heart. Captain Byrne stood beyond the door, leaning against the wall as though he had been waiting for her.

He pushed away and approached with a smile. "The noble class always displays such generous magnanimity, even when their fondest wish is to tear you to pieces. Is it an inborn trait, or do you learn it as children?"

His good cheer never faltered, but a steely glint lingered in his blue eyes. Magdalena refused to let him intimidate her. "Do you address all nobles like this, or only the ones who hold an apprenticeship?" Rather than wait for a response, she swept past him.

"You're different than they are," he said, falling in step beside her. "Not a single soul in that room would have accepted a role of servitude—except maybe the prince, but he would have done it for a lark."

She suppressed a laugh at this apt observation of Finnian's character, focusing instead upon the remark that elicited it. "Not a single soul in that room has an ounce of magic in them. I have different expectations to meet—for my own good as well as any healer's code of conduct."

"For your own good?" Cynicism crept into his expression,

as though he had finally found the hidden, conniving streak within her.

Magdalena stopped in her tracks and leveled a glare at him. "Are you familiar with empathy magic at all?" He squinted, but said nothing. "When I was eight, one of the gardeners here tripped and fell on a rake. I saw it happen. I *felt* it happen, like a spike shoved through my leg. And nobody could understand why I was crying, because there was nothing outwardly wrong with me."

He swallowed.

She drove home her point. "Every bruise and cut and scrape and scar tells a story. People get hurt all the time. The body can subdue the pain of a physical injury, but empathy magic magnifies it. If I can't control it, I am subject to it. So yes, my studies at the seminary, and my apprenticeship here, and any other education I receive have always been and will always be for my own good."

Her words hung upon an otherwise silent corridor. Captain Byrne ducked his head and said, "My apologies, milady."

Not a fragment of skepticism or insincerity colored his words. Magdalena squashed her instinctive regret.

"I forgive you," she said. "And really, I can't blame you for assuming ulterior motives. All of the nobles have them." On that quip, she continued up the hall. Captain Byrne let her go, which was only right: the prince was his true responsibility.

That night she ate her supper in her room, the tiny chamber that she had somehow managed to keep. Master Asturias had a whole bookcase crammed with tomes upon tomes of fay and magic lore. Magdalena, with his grudging permission, took a volume about sea magic with her. The prince's description, coupled with the creature she had witnessed at the cove, pointed toward a supernatural entity. She lay in bed reading about potion ingredients and sea-fay until her candle guttered against its base. When she blew out the light, shimmering waters danced through her mind and filled her dreams.

A bloodcurdling shriek pierced the dawn.

Magdalena awoke with a sharp inhale. She tore from her bedding, her legs in agony as though someone had shredded them with a dozen serrated knives. She tried to rein in her writhing magic, but to no avail. Her stomach heaved and her vision jittered with black spots and images of waves crashing against slick, dark rocks.

The pain consumed her. She dragged herself to the hall, the infirmary her only possible hope for relief, but she collapsed in a pile before she had gone more than a few yards.

Contain it. Contain it.

Tears streamed down her cheeks and pattered to the stone floor. She gulped back a squeaking sob, her throat tight and her eyes shut. As the excruciating moments passed, the fiery pain ebbed. Her legs tingled with numbness in the aftermath.

Footsteps pounded toward her. "Milady, are you all right?" Someone knelt beside her, touched her shoulder, and spoke with alarm.

She raised her head—heavy and fogged—and peered through bleary eyes at Captain Byrne. Her voice wavered. "It's passing. Please, I'll be all right."

Gingerly he helped her sit up against the wall. "I'll get someone. Master Asturias."

"No," she said and drew a gasping breath. "It only took me by surprise. But someone else is hurt. Someone else—their legs—" She paused, the memory pulsing through her. "I don't know what happened. Something powerful. Something destructive."

"Can I help you to your chamber?"

Her senses sharpened. She sat in this quiet hall, wearing her nightgown, with her hair tumbled around her shoulders and her face streaked with tears. Self-consciousness shot through her.

"I can make it there myself."

"I don't think you should—"

"Someone is hurt. Shouldn't you find them?"

He glanced up the hall. "I think I had better help you first."

A protest erupted from her lips. Heedless, he scooped her up from the floor and carried her the short distance to her own bed. "Forgive me, milady," he said as he deposited her upon the mussed blankets. He left as quickly as he had come. His footsteps echoed down the hall at a run. Magdalena stared in wonder at the empty doorway.

The longer she sat, the better she felt. A fuzziness lingered at the edges of her thoughts, but she rose and washed her face according to her usual routine. Her hands quivered as she dressed and pulled her hair into its customary braided bun. By the time she stepped cautiously out into the hallway, she felt almost normal again.

She went straight to the infirmary, hopeful that someone had found the victim of her episode. But only Master Asturias was within.

He observed her entrance with attentiveness, taking in her every move. She gathered that Captain Byrne had reported the incident. The healer said nothing, however, and when she asked whether he had seen any patients yet this morning, he only shook his head and returned to his work.

Within the hour, a tumult arose in the palace. Servants bolted past the infirmary door, exchanging whispered words. Magdalena abandoned her studies to check the hall, her heart pounding in her chest.

"What's happened?" she asked a page in transit.

The boy slowed his pace, walking backward as he conveyed the news. "The prince discovered a castaway on the ocean steps, naked as a newborn and silent as death. They're bringing her up to Master Asturias now. They say she's the prettiest little thing anyone's ever laid eyes on."

Confusion laced through her. Dazed, she turned back to the infirmary and the healer who governed it. He already prepared his examination table to receive this pretty foundling.

From further down the hall, voices chattered, their volume rising. She peeked out the doorway and glimpsed Finnian with Captain Byrne by his side and a string of curious onlookers in his wake. The prince carried a bundle in his arms, silver and blue wrapped together. As he neared, Magdalena discerned the profile of a face against his shoulder and a hand that clasped his collar tight. The blue was a blanket, and the silver that tumbled around it was mounds upon mounds of platinum-colored hair.

Magdalena's breath caught in her throat. The page had been right: this foundling was the prettiest girl she had ever seen: fifteen or sixteen years old, pale skin, a delicate frame, and a lovely face. The prince with his dark hair and strong arms looked positively heroic as he carried the wilting creature. They suited one another, like the moon suited the starry night sky.

A treacherous sense of defeat stabbed through her, but she clamped her emotions shut. She was an apprentice here. She expected nothing more.

Prince Finnian swept past her with a speaking glance. He deposited his bundle on the examination table, but when he tried to move away, the girl clung to him. She looked up with limpid blue eyes, her perfect lips never uttering a sound but every other part of her pleading for him to stay.

"It's all right," he said, gently extracting her grip from his shirt. "You're safe here. I won't let any harm come to you." After another fleeting glance toward Magdalena, he addressed Master Asturias. "I found her unconscious on the ocean steps. She hasn't said a word. I don't know where she came from or whether she's injured."

"If you would be so kind as to dismiss our audience at the door, I will examine her," said the healer.

The crowd, nobles and servants together, dissipated on the prince's command. Captain Byrne remained, but Magdalena set up a screen to block his view of the exam. Master Asturias checked the girl's vitals and inspected her body for injuries while Finnian held her hand and self-consciously looked another direction.

"She appears whole, your Highness. Open your mouth, young lady."

The girl edged closer to the prince. Her large eyes brimmed with fear.

"I don't think she understands you," said Finnian.

"Magdalena." The healer beckoned his apprentice. "A quick look should be enough."

"I don't think that's—" Captain Byrne began from the other side of the screen.

"Can you do it?" the prince asked her directly. Concern colored his words, but she could not distinguish whether it was for her or for the lovely girl that hung upon his arm. Had Captain Byrne reported her episode to him?

"Of course," Magdalena said, her voice barely above a whisper.

The foundling's sapphire gaze turned possessive as she approached. The slender limbs wrapped more firmly around the prince's forearm, and the silver head leaned into the crook of his elbow, as though daring Magdalena to attempt separating them.

She locked gazes with the girl and raised tentative fingers to her face. She brushed against her cheek. The light touch triggered a flash of images: watery darkness, punctuated with dim fairy lights; weeds and writhing serpents; a potion that glittered in its vessel like a collection of stars; a slim, sinister silhouette and the flash of a knife that sliced through flesh and muscle, leaving a trail of blood floating across her vision.

Magdalena jerked away and clapped a hand over her mouth, doubling over. Her tongue seared and her eyes watered. Finnian started toward her, but the foundling tightened her hold upon him, arresting his movement. Master Asturias looked on in alarm, and Captain Byrne rounded the screen to lay a comforting hand on her back. She shied away from him.

"No. I'm sorry, please." She pulled her wits together, painfully aware of the eyes upon her. She met only the deep blue gaze of the foundling, who stared in motionless silence.

Something about those images was off, otherworldly. The darkness; the strange, tiny lights; the pattern of inky blood floating upon the air…

"What did you see?" Prince Finnian asked.

The pain was subsiding. Magdalena forced her mouth to work, though her breathless voice wavered. "She has no tongue. Someone cut it out."

As one body they looked to the beautiful foundling. She stared forlornly up at the prince, as a child seeking compassion.

He met her gaze as he asked Magdalena, "Was there nothing else? No other injuries?"

The mutilation of the girl's mouth had pushed to the forefront of her magic, so keen that she had not checked beyond. She swallowed, steeling herself for a second glance. "I did not see. I can look again."

"No," Finnian and Captain Byrne said at the same time. The prince frowned at the captain, who solemnly shook his head.

"If the cut tongue posed a danger to her, her mouth would be bleeding," said Master Asturias. "Either the wound is old or it was cauterized, but without looking directly at it, I cannot tell. Your Highness, if you would like to leave her here for observation—"

The girl tightened her hold on the prince's arm and pressed herself more firmly against his side. Any question of whether she could understand them dissipated in that movement.

"I think she wants to stay with me," Finnian said. He glanced toward Magdalena and toward Captain Byrne beside her. To the master healer he said, "If it's all right with you, I think I'd better keep her close."

Master Asturias tipped his head. "As you please."

"Can you walk?" the prince asked the silver-haired foundling.

She lovingly smiled up at him and hopped from the table where her legs dangled. As her feet touched the ground, Magdalena gasped. Pain like a sword shot from the floor, piercing through her heels and into her legs. Quick hands caught her as she collapsed. Captain Byrne lowered her gently to the marble tile, but Magdalena only stared in horror at the foundling girl who yet stood beside the prince.

Finnian stepped forward in concern, and the foundling matched his movement. That stabbing sensation shot up Magdalena's legs again.

How was the girl still standing in such excruciating pain? How could her expression remain so serene?

Magdalena ignored the tumult of voices asking her questions. She pushed her magic outward, desperate to understand the nature of this phantom injury.

And the glamour slipped. The pale, perfect legs beneath the blanket became shriveled stumps, torn and scaly flesh that bore the pain of pressure they could not naturally support. Magdalena's mouth went dry as she locked gazes with the girl. Bulbous eyes in a noseless face peered back at her, the wide, full-lipped mouth shut to conceal the needle-sharp teeth within.

She could not breathe. She could not speak.

"*Milady*," Captain Byrne said beside her. Her magic snapped back in upon itself. The monstrous visage became beautiful once more.

"She… she…" Magdalena struggled against a tightened windpipe.

"What is it?" Finnian asked, concern infusing his voice.

The words would not come. Magdalena forced them out.

"She really is the prettiest little thing. Really, the prettiest—"

Terror raced up her spine. Whatever spell possessed this creature was potent beyond measure. Its binding magic would not allow her to speak anything but that simple, deceitful phrase.

Chapter Seven

THE PRINCE CALLED his foundling Lili. The palace, servants and nobles alike, approved.

"Such a lyrical name. It matches her graceful, delicate step."

"Have you ever seen someone move so exquisitely? It's as though she floats more than she walks."

"She really is the prettiest little thing."

The glamour stuck to the girl like a second skin. Magdalena could not get within twenty feet without experiencing the stabbing pains in her own legs, as though she walked upon knives instead of marble. The magic of the spell overrode any control she had learned through her six years of study and practice. She kept to the infirmary and her small chamber as much as possible.

"Jealous," nobles and servants alike whispered. "She's no longer the prince's favorite, and jealous to the gills."

But jealousy could hold no place in her heart when terror took up every small corner. What did such a creature want with the prince? What did it intend by coming here? Had it placed Finnian under a spell?

The foundling shadowed him wherever he went. She danced for him during his meals and slept on a pillow outside his bedroom door. Magdalena yearned to warn him of the creature's true form, but no opportunity to speak existed, and the only words the glamour allowed her to utter were praises to the girl's beauty.

"You look pale," Captain Byrne said, falling in step beside her a week after the foundling appeared.

Magdalena spared him a sidelong glance. "I was up all night reading."

"Oh? Reading what?"

She held up Master Asturias's volume on sea lore. She had combed through it so many times already that she could quote certain passages by heart.

The captain looked dubious. "Anything interesting there?"

She paused in the hall and flipped to a page near the back. Alongside the handwritten text was a sketch of a gaunt creature with bulbous eyes and a wide, sharp-toothed mouth. Its spindly arms had webbing between the fingers, and the lower half of the body narrowed into a long, scaly fin.

Captain Byrne recoiled, repulsed.

"This was the creature at the cove," said Magdalena, choosing her words carefully to avoid invoking the glamour's influence, "the one I saw, the one the prince described that night on the ocean steps."

He leaned close to read the caption. "A sea-fay?"

"Also called a siren, a lorelei, or a mermaid. It's a type of fairy bound to the ocean. This creature may have saved the prince's life."

"That's good then," he said.

She shook her head. "The folklore says they lure men into the water and drown them. Why would it bring him to the shore instead?"

"Maybe the folklore is wrong."

"Maybe." She shut the book and resumed her walk. When the captain followed, she asked, "Shouldn't you be with the prince? I thought you were his official chaperone."

"He's still in his rooms. He promised to remain there until I returned."

Skepticism flitted through her. "And you believed him?"

"Ordinarily I wouldn't, but he wanted me to check on you, so I trust he'll wait for my report. He said he hasn't seen much of you lately. You've certainly made yourself scarce."

Her heart thudded erratically in her chest. She retreated into the safety of the rules. "Does he have you check on all the ladies of the court?"

Captain Byrne barked a laugh. "He told me you might ask that. But of course he doesn't. He's worried about you."

So worried that he fused himself to a glamoured creature from the deep. Her cynicism destroyed any warmth the captain's words brought. "He should worry about himself, not me."

"Of course he worries about you. Even *I* worry." He dipped his head to catch her expression, and his voice dropped in volume. "Have you had any more episodes?"

She stared at the ground beneath her feet, unable to answer the question. She'd experienced nothing as painful as that dawn attack where she had collapsed in the hallway, but the sensation of walking on knives still elicited tears. The mysterious charm upon the foundling blanketed the whole palace, as far as she could discern, so there was no point trying to explain what pain she experienced. She would fail to form the words upon her tongue.

Captain Byrne broke the silence she had fallen into. "Milady?"

An idea occurred to her. She looked up and attempted to speak the truth. What came out instead was, "The prince's foundling really is the prettiest little thing. The prettiest. She's the prettiest little thing."

He looked at her as though she had lost her mind. "Yes. I've... noticed."

"No," said Magdalena. "She's the *prettiest little thing*."

Captain Byrne frowned. "I know."

"She *really* is the prettiest thing."

He looked annoyed. "I've got it. Can we talk about something else now?"

"I can't," said Magdalena flatly.

They paused outside the door to the infirmary. Captain Byrne studied her with a deepening furrow between his brows. "You can't?"

"I can't. Can you?"

He tossed his head. "I can talk about a lot of things."

"About the prince's foundling?"

The studious expression returned. "What's there to talk about? She's the prettiest little thing. Although, it does annoy me that she's the prettiest little—" His voice cut in his throat. He held up one hand as confusion descended upon his face. "Hang on. That's not what I meant to say. She's the prettiest little thing. No. The prettiest—"

A faint sense of triumph laced through her. She leaned in and whispered, "You can't either. No one can."

Panic danced across his face. "Why?"

Because the glamour won't allow it, she longed to say. Instead, "Because she's the prettiest little thing" pushed past her lips. She shook her head to clear it. "I think you get the point."

Dazed, he nodded.

Magdalena looked down at the book she cradled against her. "I can't find the reason why a sea-fay would pull a human to shore. If I could find that, things might be clearer."

"Are the two connected?" Captain Byrne asked.

"Of course they are," she said. "The prince's foundling is the prettiest little thing." She thumped the book, and the captain frowned.

"You mean she's—" He paused, consternation crossing his face. "I'm just going to say that irritating phrase again, aren't I."

"It seems that way."

"All right. But I think I've caught your meaning, strange as it is."

"Will you tell the prince?" Magdalena asked, anxiety building in her throat.

He tipped her a salute. "I'll try. From the conversation we've just had, I doubt that I'll succeed. Good day, milady."

She returned his farewell and stepped into the infirmary. The captain's footsteps retreated down the hall, a quick tap-tap-tap that punctuated the morning air.

In the corner, Master Asturias raised his head from where he hunched over his work. "Have you brought back my book at long last?"

"Yes. Did you want it?"

He harrumphed. "I always want my books."

She placed it on the workbench, within his reach. "And there's nothing else about ocean magic, or about the fay that live there?"

"We're lucky to have that record. Most of the tradition surrounding the fay was oral, not written."

Magdalena contemplated him as he studiously ignored her. At long last she inquired, "Master Asturias, why might a sea-fay carry a human to land instead of drowning him?"

He looked up at her through the magnifiers perched on his nose, his eyes huge in the thick lenses. "A siren that spares a human? Rare, but not unheard of. The sea-fay don't drag a man to his death because they want to kill him. They do it because they're fascinated and want to keep him as a plaything."

She pulled up a chair and settled next to him. "Fascinated?"

Annoyed, he returned his attention to his work. "The fay—both land and sea types—love humans the way that humans love cats or dogs. Every so often, one of the sea-fay remembers that her coveted pet can't breathe under water, and she returns him to shore before it's too late. It's rare, as I said."

"But why would humans fascinate them?"

"We have the advantage of a soul, and they do not."

Her heartbeat quickened. She flattened her hand upon his work table and leaned close. "How can anything living not have a soul?"

He stilled in his work. Magdalena, intent upon receiving an answer, did not avert her gaze.

Grudgingly the master healer said, "It's not that they have no soul, but that they share one collectively with all of nature. The fay are made of earth and its elements. The sea-fay are little more than brine and bone and a scrap of soul that tears from the collective when they are born. When they die their body disintegrates into sea foam and their piece of soul absorbs back into its greater whole. Do you see? The fay only exist as long as they're alive. Humans continue on as individual spirits after we die. So, we fascinate them."

Magdalena's skin crawled. "Where did you learn this?"

He blinked, the action owlish in nature. "The oral tradition still survives if you listen to the proper sources."

"Do those traditions ever speak of fay who masquerade as humans?"

His fingers tapped impatiently. "There are stories, yes."

She ignored the movement, her anxiety giving way to excitement. It seemed the glamour had no effect upon her words if she spoke in general terms instead of referencing the prince's foundling. Carefully she asked, "What about sea-fay?"

But Master Asturias shook his head. "Sea-fay have no legs. Fay magic allows a façade, but it doesn't truly transform. A sea-fay wouldn't get very far with such a masquerade beyond the waters, not with nothing but a tail fin to support its weight."

The shriveled stumps of the sea creature flashed before her eyes. A chill shot through her breast. "But what if it could somehow split its tail?"

"That would involve powerful magic—blood-based and forbidden even to the fairy denizens. And the price would be astronomical, far above what most are willing to pay. The sea-fay have no cause to sacrifice so much, to leave their ocean home to walk on dry land."

"But what if—"

"Fay magic trades pain for power, Magdalena. The price for such a spell would be constant agony. Now, if you please…" He gestured to the ingredients strewn across his table, a half-mixed potion that required his full attention.

Obediently she withdrew. Her voice lowered to a murmur. "Thank you for humoring my questions."

His gaze followed her as she settled in her own corner of the room. "If you think the prince's foundling—"

"She's the prettiest little thing," Magdalena said over her shoulder. The words rolled effortlessly off her tongue.

Master Asturias mulled over them. "Yes," he said with a frown. He returned to his work and silence governed the infirmary.

She contemplated the foundling throughout the day. She knew little of blood-based magic, except that spells cast with it had to run their course. Human sages forbade its use, but that the fay did as well spoke of its danger. Her anxiety for the prince compounded the longer she considered the implications.

This sea creature walked on dry land under a powerful, painful glamour, and she clung to Finnian like a leech. What did she hope to gain from the venture?

As evening fell, a heavy book landed with a thump on her work table. Magdalena looked in wonder from its battered leather cover to Master Asturias, who had delivered it.

"That one discusses general fay lore," he said. "Perhaps you can sate your curiosity in its pages."

She traced a finger along the cracked, weathered spine. "Thank you."

"You can be done for the night. I'll clean up."

She glanced over the raw ingredients spread upon her table. The allure of this new book overrode her inclination to leave a pristine work space. With a grateful nod, she hugged it to her and vacated the infirmary.

Her feet couldn't move fast enough. The sooner she arrived at her room, the sooner she could search for more information. The anxiety that had steadily gathered within her stretched tight.

As she approached her door, though, a figure pushed from the wall and blocked her path. Captain Byrne smiled wanly down upon her in the dimness of the hall.

"Milady," he said.

She peered impatiently past him to the refuge she had almost attained. "Shouldn't you be with the prince?"

"He went to bed early. His Majesty the king wishes to speak with you tonight."

Alarm spiked in her heart. "King Ronan, with me? Why?"

But of course, he couldn't simply *tell* her. "This way, milady." He gestured up the corridor. She dug in her heels.

"I need to put this in my room," she said of the book in her arms.

Captain Byrne hesitated, as though a fifteen-second delay might cost him his position. "Be quick about it."

Magdalena slipped inside and dropped the book on her bed, then exited to the hall again and shut her door tight. The captain motioned her to walk ahead of him.

"What's this about?" she asked as they went.

"His Majesty will explain."

The secrecy ate at her. Perhaps the king had heard from her father. Perhaps he was sending her home to Ondile. The fate of his son, the prince, weighed heavy on her mind. Would a wedding announcement soon follow her home? And if so, what would be the outcome of a marriage between human and fay?

She entered the throne room, a close, formal space rarely used. Located in the oldest part of the palace, it possessed an ancient atmosphere. Generations upon generations of monarchs had governed Corenden from the magnificent chair upon which King Ronan sat. Queen Orla beside him looked no less imposing.

Magdalena dropped into a curtsey. As she rose, she noted the absence of guards or servants other than Captain Byrne. "You wished to see me, your Majesty?"

The king exchanged a glance with his wife. She nodded her encouragement. He cleared his throat. "You have not attended many palace events since your arrival."

Magdalena interlaced her fingers and willed her heartbeat to calm. "I came here for an apprenticeship, your Majesty."

"It would please us if you attended meals in the banquet hall from now on. Master Asturias can spare you during those hours."

Her breath caught in her throat. Lili danced at the banquets. Magdalena had heard the servants talk of the foundling's grace and beauty. Her shoulders tensed at the prospect of phantom daggers punching upward from the ground.

She could no more attend those meals than she could stab her own feet.

"Forgive me, your Majesty, but—"

"I owe it to your father, the Grand Duke, to see that you attend such functions. We cannot have the daughter of our closest ally cloistered away in the infirmary while lesser nobles partake of our hospitality."

"I can't—"

"You must," Queen Orla interjected. The desperation of her voice caught at Magdalena's heartstrings.

The king reached for her hand. "My dear—"

"Ten days ago, we believed our son lost to the open sea," she said, as though she hadn't heard him. "A week ago, he vowed he would court the girl who found him on the shore."

Surprise tumbled over Magdalena like a bucket of upended water.

"And now," the queen concluded. "Now he keeps exclusive

company with a pretty child of unknown origins. What is to become of the crown of Corenden if its heir throws himself away on an inferior alliance?"

Something clicked in Magdalena's mind. The apprenticeship. Captain Byrne's remarks when they first met. The queen, without stating it outright, implied that Magdalena should draw Prince Finnian back from his infatuation with the lovely foundling. But they had sought to keep him separate from other young women as well—herself included.

"Did you not consider me an inferior alliance a mere week ago?" she asked, her voice barely above a whisper.

Queen Orla snapped her mouth shut. A blush stained her cheekbones in two bright, symmetrical spots. Her husband had no such embarrassment.

"When we believed you to be a peasant, of course we did. As daughter of the Grand Duke of Ondile, you have the proper pedigree—"

"But you still didn't approve," she interrupted, shocked at her own boldness.

He stiffened upon his throne. "We have vested interest in our son not throwing himself away on a fleeting infatuation. If his affection for you had proved lasting—"

"What affection? He has never treated anyone with special favor." Captain Byrne laid a warning hand on her arm, but she shook it off. "If I'm not mistaken, you brought me here—apprenticed me—to demonstrate how unsuitable I was to receive courtship from a prince. You should have just left me at the sage's seminary."

King Ronan pursed his lips, perfectly at ease to be frank. "We couldn't. He said he would go to you there."

Magdalena blinked at the nonsensicality of this revelation. If Finnian had truly intended courtship—which went against everything she thought she knew of him—he had a funny way of showing it. And that his attention could so quickly shift away from her again crushed her heart to pieces. She fought the despair that bubbled within her.

"We might have handled things better," Queen Orla said. "You must understand, my child: people have machinated over Finnian's marriage since the day he was born. Of course we have to be careful. It's more than his heart at stake, but the whole country, the allies that depend upon our strength. A king who makes a disadvantageous marriage presents a picture of weakness. This girl, whoever she is, cannot even speak her mind. Her tongue has been cut like a common slave's. Is she fit to ascend to the throne alongside our royal son?"

Magdalena hardened her heart. After all of his parents' interference, it would serve them right if he did marry a glamoured sea-fay. "That would be the prince's decision to make."

It was the wrong thing to say. The king's expression shuttered, and he retreated into the formality of his office. "Magdalena of Ondile, by order of the crown of Corenden, you will attend palace events from this day forward. Our son yet worries over your welfare, even in the midst of his infatuation with this unknown foundling." Magdalena glanced to Captain Byrne, from whom this detail must have emerged, but he kept his gaze rigidly forward. King Ronan continued his decree, a bite of sarcasm in his voice. "If you succeed in securing his attentions away from the pretty little castaway, you will have our blessing to marry."

Her careful upbringing allowed her to contain the scoff that fought to escape her throat. More than anything, she wanted to cry, but she wouldn't do so here, before these witnesses. She swallowed the emotions and asked in a steady voice, "And if I refuse?"

"We send you home to Ondile in disgrace and question whether our supposed ally truly honors the sovereign crown that has for generations sheltered it."

He would punish not only her but Ondile itself. Returning to her parents in disgrace she might endure, but she could not hazard destroying the ancient treaty with Corenden. The larger nation, their most important ally, had sheltered the tiny duchy from invasion and calamity.

The queen and the captain, her only witnesses to this threat, made no attempt to protest it. Magdalena dropped into a grudging curtsey. "Be it as the king commands."

Upon his throne, King Ronan actually sagged with relief. "Finnian indulges this girl because they share a common experience, both lost at sea and washed ashore. But he shares a common experience with you as well. Call that to his memory, and we shall see whether he would rather have a speaking lady of noble birth or a pretty child who can't utter a word."

She inclined her head, mute herself in this moment of despair.

"And Magdalena," he added, his voice severe, "tell no one of this meeting or what was said."

With no witnesses other than his wife and his captain, he might rescind his promises. Magdalena, sick at heart, could only accept the command.

Chapter Eight

SILENCE GOVERNED THE WALK back to her room, until Captain Byrne could bear it no longer.

"I'm sorry. It's usually my job to draw unworthy females away from the prince."

Magdalena regarded him with somber eyes. "So I gathered."

"He knows it, too, if you think me underhanded, and most of the time he approves."

"Only most of the time?"

He tipped her a smile. "I told you once that you were a special case. You had no clue, did you."

It wasn't a question.

Magdalena turned away and continued on her path, battling emotions that threatened to spill over at any moment. The prince had intended courtship based on the happenstance of her finding him washed ashore? It never would have lasted. He would have changed his mind and withdrawn his attentions.

So why did she feel as though someone had offered her the most precious desire of her heart only to snatch it away again? What would have happened had the glamoured sea-fay never appeared on the ocean steps?

She boxed her feelings and picked up her pace. Captain Byrne matched her stride. "It's likely that the king will have me escort you to the banquet hall from now on. But it's only for lunches and suppers. Your mornings will still be your own."

Unshed tears stung her eyes. She angled her head away from her walking companion in hopes that he wouldn't notice.

"I am sorry," Captain Byrne said again, ducking in an attempt to catch her gaze. "Lili will have nothing to do with anyone who's not the prince. His parents are getting desperate. And if what you indicated this morning is true, if she really is the prettiest—" His voice broke off in frustration.

Magdalena looked up, anger flaring. "What if she is? What is the outcome of a union between human and fay?"

Captain Byrne recoiled. "I... I don't know."

Shocked that the glamour had allowed such a question to pass her lips, she reined in her ire. "Neither do I. But if he loves her, let him have her. I don't want someone whose heart is elsewhere."

Her own heart screamed its protest, but she ruthlessly squashed it. They had arrived at the head of her corridor. Magdalena raised one hand to prevent the captain from following her further. "I can go on my own from here."

"But—"

"I'm not going to vanish into the night, if that's what you're worried about. I understand my duty to Ondile, if nothing else."

He stepped back with a nod, allowing her this small request. Magdalena walked stiff-backed to her room, well aware that he observed her until she slipped behind her door and shut it tight.

The moon cast deep shadows upon the tiny space. She leaned her back against the wood and inhaled a shuddering half-sob, her hands folded protectively around herself.

Even as her face crumpled and the first tears streaked down her cheeks, a scuffling sounded from the corner. A form detached from the shadows. Magdalena shrieked and scrabbled for the door handle. A hand clapped over her mouth.

"Sh-sh-shh! Malena, it's only me."

If anything, her alarm multiplied. She wrenched back, stumbling against her trunk in the darkness. "Your Highness? What are you doing here?"

She hadn't seen him in a week. He had intended courtship before his foundling washed ashore. A man had no business in an unmarried woman's room, especially in the dead of night. These and a dozen other thoughts tumbled through her brain at once.

Finnian, meanwhile, had caught her by the shoulders. "I didn't mean to startle you. It was safer to wait for you in here instead of outside, that's all. Someone might have seen me, and then word would get back—"

"Why were you waiting for me?" she blurted. Her face burned. Only moments ago, she had openly consigned him to the arms of a glamoured siren. Had he overheard the conversation down the hall? Did he know his parents had summoned her tonight, or the charge they had laid on her?

The prince withdrew a pace. Her eyes, adjusting to the darkness, caught a hint of regret in his expression. "Why shouldn't I wait for you? I was finally able to sneak out of my room without anyone noticing. Where else would you expect me to go and not get caught?"

She slipped into the safety of her cynicism. "Do you visit all the ladies of the court after dark, then?"

He scoffed. "You would ask that. No I don't. And don't put on a missish act. It's not as though you're in your nightgown—as you were when my own bodyguard discovered you last week."

Heat flared to her face. "That was—"

"Not your fault, I know. Malena, I don't want to fight. Just, please. I only wanted to see you with my own eyes."

Her pulse quickened. "Why?"

Would he admit to anything? What reason could he possibly give—?

"Because the last time we met, your magic had you snared in a terrible agony."

The concern in his voice crushed her spirit. This was the kind, compassionate boy from her childhood, the prince who cared for everyone equally, who captured hearts with a charming smile and a gentle word.

Magdalena steeled herself against the onslaught of dismay this recognition brought. "You *can't* be in my room, your Highness. It's not proper."

Silence fell between them.

"Come with me, then," said Finnian in the hush.

Her breath caught in her throat. His fingers closed around hers and he pulled her to the door.

"Where are we going?" she asked as he peeked out at the dim hallway beyond.

"The ocean stairs. The patrols in that part of the palace are sparse, especially at night."

He opened the door wider, and a shaft of light fell across her bed, where lay the text of fairy lore. Magdalena spared it a regretful glance but allowed him to draw her from her room. There would be hours enough to study when she returned.

They tiptoed through darkened corridors, illuminated only by the light of the moon from windows above. Twice they stopped in shaded alcoves for palace guards to pass; they arrived unmolested at the pavilion, where a cold ocean breeze welcomed them.

Finnian shut the double doors behind them. He squeezed her hand and led her to the steep stairway, where they settled on the top step, as they had a week ago. The waves glittered beneath the lovely moon, but far from indulging romantic fantasies, Magdalena folded her arms around her knees and wished she had brought a blanket. The king's edict echoed in her ears. Though she had not orchestrated this meeting, she felt underhanded in the prince's presence.

"Where is your foundling tonight?"

"Sleeping outside my bedroom door, as she always does."

He stared out at the ocean. Magdalena could read nothing in his expression. "How did you get past her?"

"I climbed down from my balcony."

Her jaw dropped. The prince's balcony overlooked the ocean, with a sheer descent into churning waters.

He spared her a sidelong grin. "It's not the climbing down that's a problem, but the getting back up. Are you worried I might break my neck and drown, Malena?" He bumped her shoulder with his own.

The shadows hid her instinctive blush. "Anyone would worry that."

Finnian laughed and shrugged. "It was a risk I had to take. She stirs if I open my door. I thought if I showed her all the fascinating things our world has to see that she might find something worthwhile to explore. But she refuses to leave my side except when I shut that door between us." He must have felt Magdalena's wide-eyed stare, for he added, quietly, "I know what she is."

"For how long?"

"Since the start, I think. There was something about her expression, about her touch upon my arm, that triggered my memory. I owe my life to the creature that saved me."

He did not directly connect his Lili with the creature. Nor did he speak as though he resented her undivided attention. Perhaps the prince actually would take a fairy for his queen, as the girls used to whisper in days of yore.

"She is the prettiest little thing," Magdalena said, sorrow weighing heavy on her.

An amused grunt sounded in the back of his throat, confirmation that he recognized the telltale phrase for what it was. "She really is. You don't mind?"

Her breath hitched. She forced a calm response. "Mind what?"

"Such a pretty little thing hanging on my arm wherever I go."

She bucked her head and looked away, the better to hide the tears that insisted on welling in her eyes. "What has it to do with me?"

He leaned in close, near enough that she could smell the soap he bathed with. "Malena."

She met his gaze and froze. How could he look at her like that—as though he cherished every last particle of her—when only seconds before he had spoken of another woman hanging on his arm? His breath mingled with hers. He was going to kiss her, and she, mesmerized, was going to let him, until—

Pain shot up her legs, a blade driven from her heel to her kneecap. She hissed and wrenched away from the ocean stairs. Instinct hurtled her toward the double doors to the hall, but she collapsed in a heap after only three steps, as though her very bones had shattered.

Finnian was at her side. "What's wrong?"

Magdalena spoke through clenched teeth, her face tight. "She's coming."

He looked to the closed doors. With a muttered curse, he scooped her from the marble tile and bolted across the pavilion, sidling up to the wall. The heavy door beside them swung inward to hide them from view. The prince's arms tightened around Magdalena, who bit her lower lip as the phantom stabbing pulsed up her legs.

The graceful foundling appeared, her attention fixed upon the ocean stairs. She glided from the entry to the open air, her every dainty step an agony. Magdalena, so focused on staying silent, barely registered when the girl descended the steps. She vanished from sight. The pain ebbed, and then it disappeared completely.

In the throes of her episode, Magdalena had tightened her arms around the prince's neck, his shirt clenched in her fists, her every muscle taut. The relief that flooded through her returned her senses with it. Self-consciously she pulled away, but though he lowered her feet to the ground, he kept tight hold upon her waist.

"Stay here," he whispered in her ear, his voice barely above the sound of his breath. His shadowed shape, visible against the night sky, moved away. She felt strangely abandoned. On impulse, she followed, careful to tread with stealth. Finnian peered over the balcony and drew his head back. Magdalena, as she joined him, hazarded a glance.

At the base of the stairs, where the water swirled and eddied, the foundling dipped her feet into the ocean waves. She gleamed a ghostly silver in the moonlight. The wind curled around her, picking up strands of her hair and swirling them.

From afar, a chittering sound carried through the night.

Magdalena clenched a hand upon Finnian's sleeve. He looked to her in alarm and then followed the line of her gaze.

Halfway to the open sea, a slick head rose from the waves. Moonlight glinted off sharp teeth and marbled eyes.

The prince drew Magdalena back into the shadows of the pavilion. Silently he pointed. Two more creatures had surfaced a stone's throw from the first. Another appeared, closer to the stairs, and she discerned two more further out.

The sea-fay observed the foundling. Lili only watched them in return, her legs in the water.

The otherworldly scene invoked a creeping terror up Magdalena's spine. There were more of them out there. Had they sent the first? Would they, too, acquire destructive glamours to leave the sea for dry land? And to what end?

Abruptly, Finnian interlaced her fingers with his and pulled her toward the door. The movement broke whatever trance had come over her. She fell in silent step beside him as they stole across the pavilion, with only the murmur of the ocean to fill her ears.

Their return through the palace halls passed in a blur. At her door, Finnian tightened his grip upon her hand. "I have to hurry. It'll be easiest to get back into my room while she's away from it." Disappointment laced through her, but he didn't immediately depart. Instead, fervently, he asked, "What happened, Malena? How did you know she was coming? Why did it cause you so much pain?"

She shook her head. "I can't tell you."

His brows drew together. "Why not?"

She took a halting breath and plunged ahead. "Because she's the prettiest little thing."

Confusion danced across his face, chased by vague understanding. He glanced up and down the hallway. Then, as if on impulse, he leaned in and kissed her cheek, close to her ear. The intimate touch swept a shiver through her.

"Stay safe," he whispered. He squeezed her hand again and was gone.

Her heart went with him. She tumbled into her room and collapsed on her bed, exhausted, hardly caring how the corners of Master Asturias's book dug into her side.

Chapter Nine

She awoke bathed in sunlight, curled around the heavy book and still dressed in her clothes from the night before. When she loosed her hair from its tight bun, her scalp ached. She ran her fingers through the long, brown waves.

Her eyes strayed to the leather-bound volume as she washed and dressed for the day. Reluctant to put her hair back up so soon after its release, she sat down on her bed and flipped open the faded cover. The book was old enough that it had no table of contents and no index. Magdalena skimmed several paragraphs, her gaze lingering on sketches of the various fay that once lived—and perhaps yet lived—throughout the world.

An ink-and-shadow sea-fay with its fishy face and long arms stared up at her from the page. Whoever had written this book had illuminated the creature with strokes of silver that caught the morning sun. The description beside it gave only a basic explanation of appearance and habitat, information which Magdalena had already acquired from Master Asturias's first book. She fanned through several more pages and stopped midway through the text.

This chapter discussed fay interactions with humans: how they longed for human pets, occurrences of changelings, and so forth. She turned the page to a new section: *Matrimony between Fay and Humankind*.

Fairies and humans, the book said, had incompatible bloodlines. Marriage between a fay and a human marked the end of that human's lineage, as any children born would be sterile, like a mule.

"There's reason enough for the king and queen to worry," Magdalena murmured under her breath. She curled up with the book in her lap and read on.

> *Fairies rarely seek such unions. Matrimony ties their lifespan to that of their human counterpart, while under normal circumstances the fairy would live three or four times as long. In the day that their human dies, so too does the fay who has entered into this marriage bond.*
>
> *Curiously, they do not disintegrate in the manner that unbound fairies do upon death. Instead, their body remains intact and must be handled as though it were a human corpse, through fire or burial. For this reason, many believe that a fairy who weds a human gains an immortal soul in the transaction.*

She muddled over this passage. It didn't make sense for a marriage bond to create an immortal soul where none existed.

The fay, according to Master Asturias, already had a scrap of soul from nature's greater collective, but could something as simple as matrimony develop that scrap into its own entity? And, if it could, wouldn't fairies scramble for such a precious prize instead of largely declining the union that could grant it?

The book had no answers. Instead, it changed subjects to discuss the rare, half-fay children and their attributes. She flipped ahead to where it delineated types of fay magic: glamours, charms, and thralls.

She might have believed the prince subject to a thrall were it not for his visit the previous night. If Lili had such an ability, she either had not yet applied it or could not maintain it for long. According to the book's descriptions, an enthralled Finnian would have never left his master's side.

She turned the page to the next heading: *Blood Magic*.

A chill raced up her arms.

> *Fairy law prohibits the use of blood magic. This powerful medium, when invoked, becomes self-sustaining. It feeds off of pain and destruction in an endless cycle that tortures its victims even as it grants them their heart's desire. Covenants made through blood magic cannot be broken except through the shedding of more blood. Humans or fay who seek this magic will pay a steep price for any spell it creates.*

A dark image flashed across Magdalena's memory: the potion that glittered like bottled starlight, and the quick, cutting motion that had torn tongue from throat. The trail of blood hadn't floated in the air, she realized with sickening dread. It had seeped into surrounding waters, like drops of ink would spread in a pool.

The foundling had given her tongue for a pair of mock legs and a glamour to hide the deformity.

A knock sounded against her door. Startled, she tumbled from her mattress and tossed the book aside to answer the summons.

Captain Byrne stood in the hall. He regarded her with concern. "Are you ill?"

"No," said Magdalena, self-consciously combing her hair to one side with nervous fingers.

"The morning is almost gone. Master Asturias says you never showed up at the infirmary."

"I was—" She glanced back at the book where it lay upon the floor. "I was reading."

His brows shot up. "All morning?"

"Does Master Asturias need me?" she asked, annoyed. "It's surely not time to go up to the banquet hall."

"You have another hour yet before that. He only worried that you never appeared, which made me worry, and I thought I ought to check before the king and queen had a chance to worry."

She dismissed the implication with a huff. "I was only reading and lost track of the time."

"Must be an interesting book."

"Fascinating," she said. She pocketed the handful of hairpins and the ribbon she had earlier discarded, and she pulled the door shut behind her.

The captain glanced dubiously at her unbound hair. Magdalena swept past him up the corridor, working it into a braid as she went.

"Most ladies have a servant to help them with that."

"Most ladies didn't live six years at a sage's seminary. No servants allowed." She tied off the end and wound it up into itself, lower on her head than the usual knot.

"That's more the fashion nowadays," he said.

She spared him a sour glance but otherwise ignored the remark. Her scalp still ached where the higher bun had pulled at it through the night. "You don't actually need to follow me to the infirmary, you know."

"I've come this far, so I might as well see the task through to the end."

"Aren't you supposed to be with the prince?"

"He's in the garden with his foundling and all the nobles of the court. I can escort you there if you'd prefer."

She dismissed the suggestion with a grunt.

"I thought not," said Captain Byrne.

True to his word, he didn't leave her side until she had passed through to Master Asturias's watchful care. The healer, far from inquiring her whereabouts that morning, handed her a stack of concoctions to mix and left her to her own devices.

She was halfway through the stack when the captain reappeared. Someone had informed Master Asturias of the king's desires. He bid her set her work aside and be on her way.

Dread pooled within her as she fell in step with the captain. Would the prince and his foundling arrive in the banquet hall before or after her? She steeled her senses, hoping to keep her magic close, to keep it from reacting to the glamour that encompassed the mute sea-fay.

Only a few nobles had arrived yet. The ladies whispered to one another behind their hands as they observed her. Magdalena, stiff-backed, followed Captain Byrne to her assigned seat near the head of the table.

"The daughter of the Grand Duke must receive the honor her position dictates," he said as he held her chair for her. She gingerly sat, her gaze fixed upon her hands in her lap. The sooner this charade ended, the better.

Nobles arrived in clusters. Magdalena, sick of their knowing glances, closed her eyes and concentrated on the simple breathing exercises meant to keep her empathy in check.

"How lovely to see you among us again, milady."

She looked across the table into the blue eyes of one of the female courtiers. A hint of a smirk turned the girl's lips upward.

Magdalena coolly inclined her head. "And you."

"They've seated you next to the prince. What an honor."

She glanced at the empty chair beside her, and her dread amplified. Of course the king would seat her and his son together. The prince's foundling, with no pedigree to speak of, would have no place at the table itself, but a pillow against the wall testified that she would not be far from him. Magdalena gripped her hands together.

"High birth has its privileges," the lady said. Unbridled jealousy danced in her eyes, but she would speak nothing more cutting. Magdalena outranked her and they both knew it.

It went unspoken that high birth also had its drawbacks. The lady, in the throes of her contempt, could not understand that this lunch would prove more painful than pleasurable to the woman she scorned.

Pain pulsed into Magdalena's heels. She angled her feet away from the floor in hopes that it would alleviate the stabbing sensations, but the phantom blades formed in thin air as easily as they formed from wood or stone. She clamped her fingers around the ornate table apron, her knuckles white as she fought to contain her magic. Tears pricked the corners of her eyes.

At the entry, a herald announced the arrival of the king and queen. The assembled nobles rose to their feet. Magdalena swallowed and did the same, daggers jutting from the ground beneath her.

King Ronan and Queen Orla appeared on the threshold. They observed her presence and spared an indulgent smile to one another. Prince Finnian came directly behind, with his foundling hanging upon his arm. The creature bounced along with a tranquil smile, as though her pain was nothing to bear.

Magdalena bit the inside of her cheek and silently begged her legs not to buckle.

Across the room, Finnian met her gaze and went white as a sheet. In an instant, before the eyes of the court, he swept his foundling off her feet into his arms to carry her. Gasps echoed across the room. The girl stared up at him with worshipful eyes.

Magdalena looked down at the gold-rimmed charger. As blissful relief swept through her, she couldn't stop the tears that slipped down her cheeks. Quickly she wiped them with her sleeve, but not before watchful eyes—the lady across the table included—had observed them fall.

The king and queen exchanged fretful glances as they took their respective seats. Finnian, with his usual charm, deposited Lili upon her pillow by the wall. She caught at him as though pleading for him to stay with her, but he gently withdrew. He settled in the chair beside Magdalena, signal for the rest of the company to sit.

She dropped all too readily. Servants converged on the table to start the meal.

Queen Orla, directly across from her son, leaned forward with a contrived smile. "We finally coaxed the Grand Duke's daughter to join us for lunch, Finnian."

His customary charm sprang to his face. "Coaxed? Or threatened?"

The queen puffed. Her husband scowled. "What do you mean, threatened?"

"Only joking, Father," said Finnian with a gleam to his eyes that belied his words. "In my experience, Magdalena's not so easily coaxed, is all. But of course it's nice to have her here." He favored her with a glance, more concern than pleasure on his face.

Magdalena allowed him a wan, apologetic smile and fixed her attention on her plate.

The meal passed at an awkward pace. Conversation buzzed around them, but Finnian acted as though she wasn't even there, and with each passing second she wished to be anywhere else. When his parents asked her questions, she answered as succinctly as possible, her voice low. Thankfully, lunch was not the multi-course affair that supper would be.

As the servants cleared away plates, a phantom blade stabbed into her heel. She hissed and crushed the napkin in her lap.

The prince whirled and with utmost charm said, "Lili, wait. Let me carry you." He excused himself to his parents. As he edged his chair backward, he met Magdalena's astonished gaze with a regretful, compassionate smile. She sat frozen in place, listening to the shuffle as he lifted the glamoured sea-fay from her cushion by the wall.

"I'm glad to carry you, my little foundling. You don't mind, do you?"

In her periphery Magdalena saw the girl wrap slender arms around the prince's neck and nestle against his shoulder. A hush fell across the banquet hall as they exited the room. The king and queen shifted their dismayed gazes from their son to the woman they had charged to engage him.

Magdalena, too grateful that Finnian had somehow guessed the source of her pain and spared her from it, patted her napkin against her lips and laid it on the table. "I should get back to the infirmary, if you please."

She took her leave from the pair of royals and practically fled the room, careless of the many gazes that followed her. The sight of Lili in the prince's arms burned upon her mind. Would she prefer the stabbing pain to that intimate image?

She honestly didn't know. Both options tore her up inside.

Chapter Ten

"AND HERE YOU ARE AGAIN," said Finnian at supper. He dropped into his chair with an open smile.

"Your parents are very persuasive," Magdalena murmured as she sat.

He leaned close, his expression turning conspiratorial. "Is that so? You must tell me their secrets."

The king and queen, overhearing this remark, twittered about how there were no secrets whatsoever. King Ronan shot Magdalena a warning glance behind his son's back. Discomfited, she fixed her attention on the soup that a servant was ladling into her bowl.

The prince had carried his foundling into the room, proof that he anticipated Magdalena's presence. As at lunch, he paid her little heed beyond the occasional comment. His parents, disgruntled, settled into their meal. As the second course appeared, a violinist struck a note from the far side of the room.

The sea-fay bounded from her cushion, and agony shot up Magdalena's legs.

"Lili, sit next to me," said the prince. "You don't have to dance every night."

The foundling left her place by the wall to kneel at Finnian's side, her worshipful gaze upon him. Magdalena fought against raw, writhing magic until the girl settled. Her napkin suffered the consequences, wrinkled and twisted in her hands.

Across the room, a string quartet played and dancers swirled, providing entertainment for the dining nobles. Far from enjoying the spectacle, Magdalena kept her eyes in her lap. She ate only a few bites of each course, and everything tasted like ash in her mouth. When the last course arrived, she shook her head to the servant who offered it to her. The dancers twirled across the marble tiles. On the prince's other side, Lili swayed longingly, with both her hands clasped around one of Finnian's. He maintained that hold throughout the remainder of the meal.

When he finished, he swept Lili from the floor and danced with her in his arms, swinging her in circles as he edged toward the doorway. Joy radiated from her beautiful, delicate face. The king and queen followed their son, perturbed. Several of the nobles left their places to dance or to vacate the room.

"You'll get used to the disappointment."

Magdalena looked up at a trio of ladies, all of them dressed in lovely, frilly pastels. "I beg your pardon?"

The one in the center tipped up her nose, a hint of satisfaction in her voice. "He's made his preferences clear. You'll only embarrass yourself and your family if you keep pursuing him."

She stood and regarded them each in turn. A sliver of aloofness marked her words. "You don't know what you're talking about."

The ladies bristled. "We only meant it as a gentle warning," said their spokesperson. "If his Highness throws himself away on a mute girl of dubious origins, there's nothing any one of us can do about it. There's no sense in you being so jealous of her, or of getting your feelings hurt every time you see them together."

"I'm not—" The words broke off in her throat. She could protest until she was blue in the face and they would never believe her, because their eyes told them otherwise. She fought tears whenever the prince and Lili appeared. Her manner, fueled by the fear of impending pain, exactly matched the way a jilted lover would act: sullen, sorrowful, tearful, shy.

Of course everyone would assume she was jealous.

"Thank you for the gentle warning," Magdalena said. Her voice hardened with aristocratic ice. "But you really *don't* know what you're talking about." She tipped her head to the trio and left. Unless the king and queen abandoned their schemes, she would need to cultivate a more open façade, one that could smile through pain—as Lili smiled through it.

In the safety of her room, she pored over the volume of fairy lore, searching for any information that might be of use. The flame that danced upon her candlewick ate away at the wax. A clock chimed the midnight hour from beyond her window.

And someone tapped a staccato rhythm against her door.

Magdalena scooted off her bed quilt, her heart quickly beating. Who would visit her so late? Surely not the prince two nights in a row.

But when she cracked open the door, Finnian pushed his way in and shut it tight behind him. He listened at the wood as her blood pressure spiked.

"What did I tell you? You *can't* be in here."

He waved aside her concern, his ear still pressed to the door. "It's only for a minute, Malena. There's a patrol due down this hall, and then we can escape."

"We? What makes you think I'm going with you?"

He spared her a reproachful glance. "You would make me pass my precious hour of freedom alone?"

She folded her arms and favored him with a stern glare.

Finnian grinned. "How are your legs?"

The inquiry caught her off-guard. Her heart skipped a beat, but she reined it back in. "Fine. How did you know?"

"I thought back to the times you were in pain and made an educated guess for what might trigger it. Why does it happen?"

"I can't tell you."

"Why not?"

"Because the words won't come out. I'm not keeping it to myself out of any sense of noble martyrdom, if that's what you thought."

One corner of his mouth kicked up. "All right. Then how did my parents coerce you into joining everyone for meals?"

"I can't tell you that either."

He grunted. "Ordered you to secrecy, did they?"

"Something like that."

"I suppose they've botched everything for me."

She studiously picked up the fairy book from her bed, a blush crawling up her neck. "I don't know what you mean."

"Come on, Malena. You're honest to a fault. Lying doesn't sit well on you. Why is your hair still up? Were you expecting me?"

"No!" Embarrassment flooded through her. She instinctively felt for the low, braided knot. "I was reading and hadn't gotten around to letting it down."

His eyes danced as he considered the reserved hairstyle. "You can let it down now."

She scoffed. "Hardly. You didn't climb out your balcony again, did you?"

Finnian shook his head. "Didn't have to. I think Lili must go to the ocean steps every night when she thinks I'm fast asleep. That means you and I have to go somewhere else. The garden, maybe?"

"Again you assume I'm coming with you."

"It's either that or I stay here with you. I'm fine either way, so you can take your pick."

If she blushed any deeper, she might burst a capillary. She dropped the book on the bed and crossed to the door. The empty hall beyond beckoned them. The prince, triumphant, kept close to her as they tiptoed down its shadowed lengths. Like the night before, he knew the timing of every patrol in the area.

"You sneak around a lot while everyone else is asleep?" Magdalena asked.

A wry smile curve up his mouth. "It's the only time I can pretend to be my own person. Come on."

They darted across an open corridor to a pair of doors that led outside. A silent breeze wafted through the nighttime garden, carrying upon it the scent of roses. Overhead the moon gleamed and stars twinkled against the inky black sky. Magdalena drank deep the scenery with a contented exhale.

"There it is," said Finnian as he ambled next to her. "Don't pretend you're not happy to be here."

She motioned to the flowering shrubs. "Who could be unhappy surrounded by all of this?"

"Does that mean you forgive me?"

She stopped short and stared. "Forgive you for what?"

"For lunch and for supper, and for meddling parents who ruin everything."

Though his bitterness was justified on that last item, she could not let it stand. "They're worried about you, your Highness."

"Can we drop the title for tonight?"

She sighed and looked the other way. "I don't see why. It doesn't change anything."

The charming smile that leapt to his face might have left her dizzy, if she were of a mind to accept it as genuine. It was easier to assume he was up to mischief, though.

"If that's true, then it shouldn't matter if we drop it," he said.

So what if he was up to mischief? The chance to stand as equals with him, if even for a sequestered hour, proved too much. She conceded the point. "Your parents are worried about you, Finnian."

"Because they don't trust me. No one trusts me. Right now you're the closest ally that I have."

She twisted her fingers together, uncertain how to respond. He saw the motion and caught her hand, drawing her attention back to him.

"I wish they'd left you out of it, Malena. For your sake. They don't understand, and you're powerless to explain. But they wouldn't understand even if you could. Do you remember when that gardener fell on his rake?"

She shuddered at the recollection. It marked the first flare of the magic that now governed her life.

Finnian pointed to a willow tree. "I sat with you over there, up against the trunk."

"You stayed with me until I stopped crying," she said. The memory, so sweet at the time, had quickly turned sour.

"And the next day, when you and the other girls squabbled over who could sit next to me at lunch, I said that we all had to be friends and that everyone had to take turns. And you never tried to sit next to me again."

Displeasure welled in her throat. She tamped it down and affected carelessness, withdrawing her hand and stepping lightly away. "Of course not. Other girls wanted it more than I did."

"No. You just have never liked to share."

Her attention snapped to his face, her heart twisting in knots.

Finnian smiled wanly. "We're cut from the same cloth, you and I. The difference is that you have the luxury of being honest, whereas I have a duty to keep the peace."

He shifted his gaze elsewhere, to the shadow-swathed trees and sleeping flowers. She studied his profile, the man that, for years, she had hated to love. "Is that your way of saying I'm ill-tempered?"

A laugh escaped his throat. "I just said we're the same, so I'd be calling myself ill-tempered too. It seemed, all those years ago, that I could always depend on you to speak aloud whatever I was thinking."

Memories assaulted her, of all the times he had drawn her into conversations and games. *"Magdalena hasn't said anything yet. We have to give her a chance to speak." "Is Magdalena participating? We can't do anything that would leave someone out."*

"I always thought you were trying to annoy me."

"I was. You kept retreating into your books and ignoring me. I don't like to share any more than you do." He plucked at a leaf on a tree, as though the casual action might buffer the words he spoke. Magdalena's nerves fluttered. Before she could respond, Finnian turned his full attention upon her.

"Malena, I know what my parents think and what everyone at court says about me. I know what it looks like. I was hoping for a quick resolution with Lili, but I don't know what she wants or why she came here."

"Don't you?" Magdalena asked.

A telltale panic chased across his face, proof that he had better instincts than he admitted.

Tidbits of fairy lore flittered through her mind, coupled with the foundling's behavior. Magdalena chose to be blunt. "I think she wants you to marry her."

Finnian recoiled. "Why—?"

"Master Asturias says that the fay have no immortal soul, but one of his books says they can gain one by marrying a human. She clearly adores you—worships you—and if she once saved your life, perhaps she hopes—"

"I'm not a trophy, thank you very much." His voice, hard as stone, cut through her explanation. Her brows arched, but he continued. "Does saving someone's life bind them to you? You saved my life when you found me on that beach. Am I bound to *you*?"

"Of course not."

"Then why should I bind myself to her?"

"I didn't say you should."

But he quickly closed the space between them and grasped her by the shoulders, as though she required further convincing. "I'm grateful—*grateful*—that she spared my life. More grateful than I could possibly express, and I have tried to repay that service with kindness. But I would sooner die than be yoked to someone out of duty."

Her memory flashed to that agonized night she had passed believing him consigned to a watery grave. She shrugged out of his grip and stepped back. "Don't say that. Life is always better than death. Your people love you and they need you. You don't know what it was like when everyone thought you were dead."

The prince's head tipped. His expression turned uncomfortably perceptive. "Did you cry for me, Malena?"

Tears prickled at the memory, and so did resentment. "Everyone cried for you."

"I didn't ask about everyone. Did *you*?"

He wanted a confession, and she wasn't ready to give it even though the answer was as plain as the sun in the daytime sky. Insufferable man.

She swatted him with the back of her hand, her eyes bleary. "Why do you think I was moping by myself in the cove that morning?" Wonder crossed his face. She babbled. "I hadn't even seen you in six years, and I felt like someone had gutted me. I can't imagine what anguish your parents and your friends here at court must have suffered. Don't talk about death being preferable. It's not, and it never will be."

She would have walked away from him, struggling to hold her tattered dignity intact, but he snatched at her elbow and dragged her into his arms. Magdalena squawked an incoherent protest, her eyes huge and her spine as stiff as a board. The embrace flooded a dozen conflicting emotions through her.

Finnian laughed into her hair. "How can you be so nice and so thorny at the same time?"

"How can you be so shameless?" she replied, her hackles raised. "Or do you go around hugging all the ladies of the court? Is that why your parents require a chaperone?"

He pushed her back to arm's length, all the more amused. "The chaperone is for my protection, not anyone else's. They won't give any lady opportunity to declare a closer relationship than actually exists."

"And yet here we are," said Magdalena, her pulse thundering in her ears. "What's to stop me from making some outrageous claim to everyone?"

But the prince shook his head. "We both know you never would. Besides, I wouldn't mind if you did, so there's nothing to worry about."

Her heart stuttered and her breath caught in her throat. She covered it with an instinctive scowl, but before she could rebuke him for flirting, he spoke.

"My parents told you, didn't they? Of my intent to court you? It can't be what induced you to torture yourself with these royal banquets, but if I know my father, that was the first lure he tried."

She stepped back a pace. "It was your mother, actually. I assumed that she misspoke."

"That hurts my feelings," he remarked to the air.

"It's—" She caught herself before anything more hurtful might emerge. Now was not the time to let her emotions reign. She took refuge in objectivity. "What was I supposed to think? You never show favor to anyone."

"Not true. Also not smart to assume I'm exactly as I was six years ago or that circumstances are the same. But don't fret about it, Malena. If the idea is so repulsive to you—"

"What are you talking about?"

He stared, his expression blank.

Her emotions, in the intimacy of the moment, refused to

be suppressed. She clutched a protective hand to her heart. "What's repulsive is this inborn fear that you're making fun of me. Courtship because I found you washed up on a beach? That makes no more sense than you marrying a glamoured sea-fay out of duty."

Finnian blinked. "It's not because you found me on a beach. I've been biding my time for ages."

"What?" she croaked.

He swept a hand behind him in a grand gesture. "*Ages*, Magdalena. You weren't supposed to be at that blasted seminary forever."

She opened her mouth but shut it again without saying a word, her thoughts too jumbled to form a coherent sentence.

"In my defense, I would have gone about it the proper way, with enough opportunity for both of us to decide whether the match was a good fit. I mean, I always knew you might reject me, but after looking death in the face, I had to at least try. And considering that it was *your* face I saw when I first opened my eyes, I thought it was the fates giving me their permission. But it's all useless now, because my parents have meddled, and there's Lili to deal with, and you seem completely appalled at the whole idea."

She cobbled together her wits. "I'm—I'm not appalled. I'm *flustered*."

He quirked an eyebrow. "That's more encouraging. So it's all right if I proceed?"

A sudden helplessness washed over her. She glanced around the nighttime garden, as if it might present a refuge to her. What did he mean by "proceed"? What kind of attention would he draw? Was this real, or had she fallen asleep in her tiny room?

And yet, she spoke a very small, "Yes."

He huffed a laugh and looked skyward. "You don't have to force yourself."

"I'm not—"

"You're overthinking things, aren't you?"

"Probably."

He laughed again, with more sincerity this time. His charm thus renewed, he caught her hand and brought it to his lips. Magdalena stared, fascinated, as he held her gaze. A shiver raced up her spine, coupled with a vague regret that he had only kissed her fingers.

"Oh. This is more promising than I thought," said Finnian, as though he could read her mind. She, too perplexed to muddle through such teasing, tried to remove her hand, but he tightened his grip and pulled her into a proper kiss.

A lovely, heart-fluttering kiss, one that shot delight through her, all the way to her toes. In its aftermath, Finnian pinned her with adoring eyes, a soft smile playing at the corners of his mouth. She couldn't stop her own lips from curving upward.

And a horribly unromantic thought occurred: where had he learned to kiss a girl with such finesse?

He saw the change in her expression, because he drew back with a frown. Before she could speak a word, he said, "Magdalena, so help me, if you ask me whether I kiss all the ladies of the court—"

"Do you?" she blurted. But she instantly held up her hands. "Don't answer. I don't want to know."

His charm turned wolfish. "Don't you?" He stepped close again and snaked an arm around her waist before she could retreat. Her breath grew short—she dared not look away—but the predatory gleam in his eyes turned laughing. "Don't be silly. I'd have a dozen scheming mamas at the palace doors demanding that I make their daughters an honest offer, and word would be all over the kingdom that I was a libertine. Which I'm not."

"Present evidence begs to differ," she said, though a giddy light-heartedness tempted her to laugh.

"Pining after one woman for years hardly a libertine makes," he quipped, and he ducked his head to kiss her again, no less expert in this second execution.

The scent of flowers and the dull roar of the ocean combined against her stubborn logic. She slid her arms around his neck and let the moment carry her away.

"What now?" she asked, her voice barely above a whisper, her eyes shut as though she might block the inevitable return to reality.

He tucked a stray wisp of hair behind her ear. "Now I try to resolve all the obstacles cluttering my life. You don't mind these nighttime meetings, do you?"

She looked up at last, a somber calm descending on her. "I don't think they're exactly appropriate."

He tipped his head to one side, considering. "Probably not. But I can't see you during the day unless I'm carrying Lili, and that defeats the purpose."

How quickly such shimmering delight could fade. The communion of a scant minute ago dissolved. "There's always lunch and supper," she said cynically.

"Where, I presume, my parents intend you to ensnare me with your feminine wiles."

"Don't laugh. It's not funny."

He tightened his arms at her waist, preventing a retreat. Concern brimmed in his eyes. "What threat do they hang over you, Malena?"

She curled her fingers around his lapel and absently studied its tailored edge. "It's not... a threat, exactly. I have a duty to Ondile and to our alliance with Corenden."

In the darkness, he grew very still. "Are you here with me now out of duty to Ondile?"

A spike of indignation lanced through her. She lifted flashing eyes to meet his gaze. "I'm here with you because you scandalously dragged me from my room in the middle of the night. And if you think I would let someone kiss me out of duty—"

But he silenced the rest of this remark by engaging her mouth in that much more pleasant pastime. The fickle euphoria returned, though she did not trust it so completely this time.

"Finnian—" she began as soon as she was able.

"I only have to convince my parents to agree. All things considered, it shouldn't take much."

"Agree?" she repeated, her mind dazed and her eyes clouded as she looked up at him.

"To let me marry you."

A sardonic chuckle escaped her lips. "Oh."

"It's not that they don't approve, exactly. They just want me to wait a couple more years."

She fought amusement. "Well, they told me if I could lure you away from your foundling, I could have you."

He drew back to regard her with mock reproach. "And you didn't even try."

The laugh escaped, though with a rueful twist. "The whole court already thinks I'm heartbroken because I'm on the verge of tears whenever she's with you. I wasn't about to add 'desperate and pathetic' to their list of charges."

He planted a matter-of-fact kiss upon her. "All right. I'll fix it."

"Fix what?"

"Everything. You will marry me, won't you?"

Her heart flip-flopped in her chest. "Yes, if you want me."

"I do. More than anything. And I must say, this courtship has gone infinitely better than I thought it would."

Too many emotions pressed upon her. Finnian swept her into a warm embrace, and the night breeze swirled its whispered approval around them.

Chapter Eleven

THE BANQUET HALL BUZZED with conversation. Cutlery clinked against plates up and down the table, and laughter twittered from the far end. Magdalena focused on her lunch, hyperaware of the prince in the chair beside her and half wondering if she had dreamed everything the night before.

Finnian had arrived behind his parents, with Lili snuggled up in his arms. After setting her on her cushion, he had taken his seat with little more than an encouraging smile to Magdalena.

Doubts and misgivings fluttered through her. At any given moment, half a dozen court ladies whispered to one another as they glanced snidely at her. Too many of them considered her defeat a personal triumph. How would they feel if the prince actually followed through with the proposal he had made in the garden last night?

She jumped when a tinkling note echoed through the room. Finnian tapped the handle of his knife against his cut crystal goblet and stood from his chair. Magdalena looked to him in alarm, but he only spared her a brief glance as he surveyed the company.

His charming smile contrasted with the stricken hush that fell. "Everyone, I have an announcement to make."

At the head of the table, the king reached for the queen's hand and gripped it tight. They both appeared as though the world was about to end, and their son seemed not to care one whit.

Finnian raised his glass to make a toast. "It is my great pleasure to announce my engagement and upcoming marriage—" Devilish soul that he was, he paused on this word and savored the pall upon the room. Magdalena stared up at him in horror as he cheerfully met her gaze and finished, "—to Magdalena of Ondile."

Gasps punctured the air, followed by a smattering of applause.

King Ronan, in a voice of mingled relief and reproof, said, "My son, should you not have told your own parents before announcing this joyful news to the whole court?"

Finnian feigned bewilderment. "I did tell you, Father. I told you ages ago."

The king turned a ruddy hue. "Have you applied to the Grand Duke, then?"

"He won't object. At any rate, the news was much too happy to keep to myself." Finnian resumed his seat. He caught one of Magdalena's hands from her lap and raised it to his lips to kiss her knuckles. His gray eyes laughed.

She could look nowhere else, too aware of the gaping nobles who, moments previous, believed her a jilted former favorite. The abruptness of the announcement, the lack of warning, all worked her heart into a tremored rhythm.

The prince leaned close and said, "I told you I would fix everything."

Conscious of the many nobles who observed their private interchange, she whispered, "How does this fix things?"

"It establishes what is real and what is not."

"But—" Pain lanced through her legs. She winced and looked to the wall. Finnian twisted toward to his silver-haired foundling.

The exquisite creature stood beside her cushion, her speaking blue eyes enormous. Her haunted expression shot a pang of terror up Magdalena's spine.

"Lili," the prince began, his voice tinged with charm.

The foundling bobbed her head, as though offering congratulations, and like a frightened gazelle, she bounded from the room. Conversations stuttered to a halt. Magdalena gripped Finnian's hand and curled in on herself until the fiery phantom blades ceased their assault. During this episode, the prince dragged his chair near and draped a protective arm around her shoulders.

"My dear, are you quite all right?" Queen Orla asked across the table.

Magdalena schooled her pain into something neutral. "Yes," she said, and she exchanged a glance with her affianced. The warmth of his apologetic eyes bolstered her.

Lunch ended soon afterward. When she attempted to return to her apprenticeship, the queen stood in her path. "So many plans and preparations to make. No, Finnian, we don't need you. Your time might be better spent applying to the Grand Duke for the permission you only assume he will give."

Before the prince could reply, Queen Orla whisked her future daughter-in-law away from the banquet hall, and away from all the waiting nobles who hovered in hopes of ingratiating themselves to their future monarchs.

"You managed things quite well," the queen said when they achieved the solitude of her private parlor. "I'll admit I didn't expect such success, and certainly not so soon."

"Nor did I," said Magdalena.

Queen Orla studied her, but whatever she sought eluded her. "Well, I won't ask how you did it. He's announced before the court that he'll have you for his bride, so it's done. The wedding shouldn't take more than a week to prepare."

Magdalena nearly choked. "So soon?"

The queen glanced her over from head to toe. "When a bride and groom live under the same roof, even a roof as large as this one, sooner is better." An enterprising gleam lit her eyes. "Unless you wish to return to Ondile for a visit before you marry…?"

"No, but—"

She waved aside the protest on Magdalena's lips. "This gives your parents enough time to travel here. Were they not coming from so far, I would have everything ready in two days instead of the week. My dear, you must know we have an army of servants at our disposal. You will make a lovely bride."

She summoned her own dressmaker that very afternoon, and by sunset Magdalena had been measured and poked and plied for a dozen opinions on fabric, lace, flowers, and refreshments, until her head spun and doubts fluttered at the edge of her thoughts.

After the dizzying session ended, she trudged through the marbled halls with every intention of holing up in her bedroom for the rest of the night. A throat cleared, and she looked to an adjoining corridor to find Captain Byrne waiting for her.

"It's almost suppertime, milady."

Magdalena's heart plummeted. "What? No. I already did what they asked of me." Indeed, when letting her go, Queen Orla hadn't even hinted at seeing her again that evening.

"As the prince's future bride, your place is with the royal family," the captain said. "Do you want to change first, or shall I escort you to the waiting area?"

She looked down at the dark gray of her dress. "Change into what?" Everything in her trunk was roughly that same cut and color. All her pretty dresses remained in Ondile.

Captain Byrne seemed to understand in an instant. "Come on," he said, and gently he led her up the hallway. Her nerves rekindled as they went. Where had Finnian spent his afternoon? Where was the foundling? Had she gone back to the sea, or did she lurk in some shadowed corner of the palace?

Or had she returned to the prince? Lili's pleading eyes flashed before Magdalena, the heartbreak within them almost palpable. She pushed away the memory and its accompanying guilt.

The waiting area, a sitting room lavishly furnished, had only dim lanterns for light. Captain Byrne ushered her inside and lengthened the wicks on those nearest the door. He was about to retreat, but he stiffened with suspicion.

"Your Highness, are you already in here?"

After a long, tense moment, a sigh issued from the depths of a wingback chair that faced the opposite direction. A pair of feet lowered to the floor. Finnian stood and turned a baleful glare upon his appointed chaperone.

Captain Byrne dutifully positioned himself by the door.

"It's not necessary for you to stay, you know."

"It's more necessary now than ever, your Highness."

Magdalena glanced between the pair, fighting the urge to laugh. Her affianced beckoned to her with wagging fingers. She joined him and took the hand he offered. He plopped back into his chair, dragging her with him.

A protest bubbled from Magdalena's throat, and embarrassment flooded her face. The chair, roomy enough for one person, did not so easily accommodate two. Finnian had her sprawled across his lap, his arm tight around her waist. She had instinctively placed hers around his neck to steady herself.

"Your Highness, show some decorum, please," said a long-suffering Captain Byrne, now out of sight by the door.

"We're engaged," the prince said over his shoulder. His stare held Magdalena's, and she could hardly breathe from the intimacy of it. "If you're going to intrude on a pair of lovers, you don't deserve decorum."

He kissed her then, a soft and captivating welcome.

A shadow fell across them, and Magdalena glanced up and then away with a deep blush.

"Yes, I was wondering about that," said the captain. Far from being ruffled by their intimate position, he seemed not to notice. "You two are a lot closer than expected, given that I've chaperoned your every encounter. Except I haven't, have I?"

A chuckle vibrated in Finnian's chest. "Go away. So help me, if ever you fall in love, I'm commanding an entire platoon to dog your steps."

Captain Byrne hummed, a cynical sound, but he did withdraw.

"Malena, pretend he's not here," the prince whispered, mischief dancing in his eyes.

"Your parents might arrive any minute now," she said. "Do you really want them to find us like this?"

He answered her with another kiss, clearly unconcerned with the king and queen's impending advent.

"Where's Lili?" Magdalena asked, breathless.

"Don't know. Couldn't find her."

"Do you think she's gone back to the sea?"

"I don't know. This is for you." He fished into his pocket and withdrew a small ring, which he slipped on the third finger of her left hand.

She looked down at the pearl that gleamed within it. Tiny, glittering diamonds flanked either side.

"It's been in the family for generations," said the prince. "It suits you."

Her heart swelled. She kissed his cheek. "It's perfect."

The door latch clicked, suspending any further intimacy. With a sigh, Finnian shifted Magdalena from his lap. They both rose, hands clasped, as King Ronan and Queen Orla entered.

"Oh!" The queen regarded the pair in surprise before her gaze shifted to her future daughter-in-law. "My dear, you did not dress for supper."

Finnian spoke before Magdalena could respond. "Why are women so concerned with their clothes? She always looks nice." He led her to the opposite side of the room. Together they settled on a small sofa. The king and queen exchanged an uncertain glance, but they were too grateful for their son's present choice of companion to make a fuss, lest he revert to the previous one.

The atmosphere of the room, stiff and stuffy, broke with the tinkling of a dinner bell. Captain Byrne opened wide the doors and accompanied the royal entourage to the banquet hall, where the nobles of the court had already assembled. Magdalena, despite her dark dress and simple appearance, stiffened her posture and entered on the prince's arm as though she were already queen.

As the servants circled with the first course, the orchestra in the corner struck the notes of a lively tune.

Phantom fire burst up Magdalena's legs.

Instinctively she clutched Finnian's forearm, her fingers digging into the folds of his coat sleeve. He looked first to her and then to the line of dancers gliding into the hall. Long, silver hair fluttered from their midst. Finnian started to rise, as though to stop them, but Magdalena jerked him down. She bit the inside of her cheek and mutely shook her head.

It would cause too much of a spectacle.

Stricken, he clasped her hand and drew his chair a fraction closer.

Every stabbing footstep Lili took raised bile in Magdalena's throat, the pain so excruciating that she could hardly stand it. The foundling danced with the grace of a swan upon the waters. Her slender arms arched and fluttered, and her feet seemed not to touch the floor. The glamour, at its brightest, most vibrant state, shielded the awful, tattered truth from view with a dazzling façade.

How the foundling managed, Magdalena could not understand. The rapture of the company, the lyrical highs of the music, faded in her ears. She curled her feet in her shoes and tried to focus on something—anything—besides the dancing girl, but every step beat like a drum against her, knives and swords shoving into her heels, shattering her bones until she could bear it no more.

And Lili danced on as though her very life depended on it.

The empathy magic expanded. Physical pain burst and flowered with heartache and grief and a precious something forever *lost*.

"Such a moving performance," said the nobleman on Magdalena's left, his eyes never leaving the graceful foundling.

"She really is the prettiest little thing," she replied, her voice a mere whisper.

Finnian pressed a handkerchief to her cheek. She turned to him in wonder and realized she was crying.

"We can leave," he uttered, too low for anyone else to overhear. "Out the side door. No one but Gil would notice us."

But his optimism on that count had no foundation. "I can't walk, not like this," Magdalena said. "And you can't carry me without drawing attention from the whole court."

Concern wore deep lines into his charming face. Magdalena, on impulse to comfort, leaned over and kissed him.

A violin stuttered, and two massive blades lodged in her heels to stay. She jerked her attention to the dance floor, where Lili stood frozen, her huge blue eyes fixed upon the couple. Despair skipped across the foundling's face as the other dancers whirled and twirled around her. Nobles up and down the table noticed her arrested movement. They looked from her to the prince and his future bride.

As at lunch, the silver-haired foundling bolted from the hall. Magdalena hissed, her grip tight on Finnian's hand, but the pain receded into numbness. The dance continued, the music soaring up to the open windows high above, where it mingled with the wind.

Chapter Twelve

"You've been exchanging letters," said Captain Byrne as he escorted Magdalena back to her room that night.

She frowned at him. "Who? The prince and I?"

"It's the only logical conclusion. Either that, or you somehow orchestrated clandestine meetings while avoiding both me and his silver-haired arm-leech. She really is the prettiest little thing."

This added phrase, Magdalena suspected, was the glamour's punishment for the insult that preceded it. Captain Byrne made a sour face but did not retract his words.

"It must be letters," he said. "Left for each other in the garden, or some such trysting place. Although, your familiarity with one another—"

"Letters, yes," she said quickly. "The prince can be quite eloquent when he wants to be." The officer spared her a cagey glance. Perhaps she had accepted his explanation too readily. She turned her attention forward. "I can go on my own from here."

"What would his Highness say if I had to report abandoning you halfway?"

"I really don't think he would mind," said Magdalena. Finnian would have escorted her himself, but his parents insisted on a private audience with him. His expression when King Ronan ordered Captain Byrne to play escort in his stead had spoken volumes on his feelings for this arrangement.

"Nevertheless, you're stuck with me until you're safe in your own room."

She gritted her teeth and kept walking. Relief flooded through her when the door came into sight, and even more so when she shut it between them. Captain Byrne could kindly take his speculation elsewhere.

Not an hour later, a tap-tap-tap drew her back to the hall. As the night before, Finnian slipped inside as soon as she cracked the door open.

"You're early," she said with some surprise.

"Lili's disappeared again. I sent Gil to look for her." He eyed her braided bun with dissatisfaction. "I take it you expected me?"

"Yes." Suspicion crossed her mind and manifested in a scowl. "You're not trying to catch me in my nightgown, are you?"

"N-no!" he stuttered, and his face turned the shade of a steamed lobster. "Of *course* not! Only—would it kill you to let your hair down? You're always as neat as a pin."

She arched her eyebrows at him. Brief temptation flitted through her mind—to give in to the simple request, to loose the heavy braid and let her hair fall in waves down her back, to observe what effect this might have upon him. But, given their surroundings and his propensity towards physical affection, she dismissed the idea.

"Come on," she said, drawing him by the hand toward the hall. "You know I don't like you in here."

"Does it worry you, Malena? We'll be married in a week." Behind his dancing eyes lurked a wariness that betrayed his own concern.

"It won't worry me when we're married," she said simply. She pulled him from her room and shut the door behind them.

They spent a lovely evening playing cat-and-mouse with Captain Byrne, who, having abandoned his search for Lili, focused instead on locating the prince. Finnian knew dozens of hidden nooks throughout the palace and delighted in dragging Magdalena from one to the next as they evaded the stalking officer.

Captain Byrne, too proud to ask his fellows for help—or too reluctant to admit he'd lost his charge—tiptoed through the palace whispering threats under his breath. He seemed at last to abandon the search, but when Finnian and Magdalena circled back to her room, he stood propped against the door waiting for them.

"Mm-hmm," he said in disapproval.

"Oh, keep your shirt on," said the prince. "We're getting married." He primly kissed his fiancée on the cheek and saw her through the door, after which their abandoned chaperone escorted him back down the hall.

Magdalena readied for bed, toying with the pearl engagement ring all the while. When it came time to blow out her candle, she left the bauble on her finger and curled into her pillow with a sigh. Sleep descended, and her thoughts drifted to ethereal realms.

"It's not a soul of your own that you'll get."

Darkness pulsed before her eyes, with the vivid awareness that only came in dreams. A shadowed creature swam from one shelf to another, collecting items as it spoke.

"Fay like us can't have our own souls. The best we can do is to latch onto someone else's, though why anyone would want that is beyond me." Sharp eyes surveyed her, and a cunning smile curved up the creature's mouth. *"But you do want it, don't you. Foolish child."*

The creature emptied its collected items into a leaden vessel. The strange fluids sank and sloshed together, denser than the water around them.

"It'll cost you. It'll cost you what's most precious to you, and if the human doesn't marry you, if he doesn't join his soul to your little scrap, you die."

Shock struck Magdalena like a thunderbolt. The creature continued on as though she wasn't there.

"Do you understand, little siren?"

"Yes." The word echoed into the water from a sweet and desperate voice.

"So we have a deal?"

"Yes."

The shadowed creature grunted. With trenchant proficiency, it sliced a jagged knife across its chest. Black blood dripped like tar into the vessel. The contents swirled and sparked with the light of a thousand tiny stars. In the aftermath, the creature smeared spindled fingers across its self-inflicted wound. The blood, thick and sticky, formed a ghastly seal.

"I'll take my payment now, my dear."

The knife slashed toward her. Magdalena jerked awake, her tongue on fire as if someone had torn it out.

Lili lay beside her on the mattress, staring solemnly at her through the pale morning light.

Magdalena shrieked and wrenched away. She tumbled off the bed, her arms flailing as she hit the floor in the narrow gap between her mattress and the wall. In horror she stared at the foundling, who knelt on all fours to peer over the edge at her.

"Wh-what are you doing here?"

Lili narrowed her eyes as if contemplating a particularly stupid child. Her silver hair tumbled around her, glossy and luxurious in the light from the window. The exquisite lines of her face—the perfect nose, the rosebud mouth—blurred and realigned. She caught Magdalena's left hand and sat back on her haunches to study it.

More specifically, to study the pearl ring upon it.

Her lovely fingers felt as cold as ice. The back of Magdalena's neck prickled with terror as the glamoured sea-fay examined the ring. When Lili moved to take it off, Magdalena clenched her hand into a fist and tugged it protectively to her chest.

Resentment crossed the foundling's face.

The vision, the shadowed creature's words—

"You need him," said Magdalena.

Lili met her gaze, her sapphire eyes teeming with fervor.

Magdalena pressed on. "If he doesn't marry you, you'll die? But why him? Can't you choose someone else?"

The foundling shook her head with such violence that her silver hair rustled around her. Her eyes burned like embers as she reached again for the ring.

But Magdalena twisted away, shielding it between herself and the wall. Ice-cold fingers scrabbled at her. She hunched into a ball, terror fluttering in her throat but her determination unwavering. The ring itself could not confer an engagement from one girl to the other, but if Lili took it, if she hid it or lost it—

"It's not yours!" Magdalena cried, anger spiking within her.

The silver-haired foundling sat back again, her mouth set at a defiant line.

Magdalena, no less defiant, said, "*He's* not yours. He's not a trophy. He's not a pet, or something you can own. I don't own him. No one owns him."

The girl frowned as though presented with a concept completely foreign to her. Magdalena looked down at the gleaming pearl and contemplated the engagement that it represented. Lili's life depended on the prince, but he had chosen another. What responsibility did Magdalena bear in this tangle?

Could she give him up to spare the girl?

"If he had chosen you, I would have accepted it. My heart would have shattered, but I would have accepted it. He's not an object. He doesn't have to meet anybody's expectations but his own."

Lili eased back on the bed, that incomprehensible expression still on her face. As her feet touched the floor, Magdalena hissed.

The foundling cocked her head. She stepped to one side, observing. The knives lanced through Magdalena's feet and summoned tears to her eyes. Lili crossed around the bed, her wide eyes taking in every wince, every pained flinch.

Magdalena's magic roiled out of control, and the foundling loomed over her, wonder in her expression.

"How do you endure it?" she asked through clenched teeth.

Lightning-quick the creature stomped her foot. A cry wrenched from Magdalena's throat. Lili stomped again and again and again, until tears flooded down her victim's cheeks. With a fierce expression, she thrust out her hand.

Magdalena, despite her misery, said, "*No*."

The foundling recoiled. Confusion danced across her face.

"It's not mine to give you."

Understanding dawned. In reluctance she withdrew. At the door she cast a resentful glance over her shoulder before passing through to the hall.

Magdalena let out the breath she had unconsciously held. The throbbing pain in her legs ebbed, but she lay in that nook between bed and wall, listening to the silence around her, terrified that the desperate creature would return.

She hadn't felt Lili enter the room. She must have been in a deep enough sleep that her magic had remained dormant.

Direct contact when the girl had climbed onto her mattress had stirred it awake, and Magdalena with it shortly thereafter.

She shuddered and half rose. Her head pounded and her vision swam. Lili knew now that her every footstep caused the prince's affianced incredible pain. What would she do with that knowledge?

A tap on the door roused her from this reverie. "Who is it?" she called, tossing a blanket around her shoulders as she stood.

"Captain Byrne, milady."

"What do you want?"

"We've come to move you to another room."

Ordinarily she would have questioned this seemingly random announcement. After this morning's encounter, she wanted nothing more than to get away from these narrow walls. "Just a minute," she said, scrambling to get dressed.

When she opened the door with her hair still tumbled around her shoulders, the captain raised his brows in teasing surprise. "Serves you right for staying out so late last night," he said, and he swept past her with a pair of underlings.

Magdalena ignored the quip as she worked a braid. "Where are you moving me?"

"To quarters among the other nobles. It's where you belong if you're going to marry the prince. Besides, it won't do for your parents to arrive and find you living in a hole like this."

"The king and queen seek not to cause offense with Ondile," she surmised.

"And the nobles' wing is better patrolled at night," he said with a cheeky wink.

The new quarters, far more spacious, featured a canopied bed and a window that overlooked the garden.

"But don't get too comfortable," said Captain Byrne. "You move to the prince's room on your wedding night."

He exited then, leaving her in a state of high embarrassment.

Chapter Thirteen

"Why, pray tell, does a mere captain keep stumbling across you with your hair down?" Finnian asked when Magdalena met him at lunch.

"How can you possibly know that?" She glanced across the room at Captain Byrne stationed by the door. From his position, he could not hear their quiet conversation, but the smug, upturned corners of his mouth indicated that he knew their topic.

"Because he keeps bragging about it to me. One of these days I'm going to grind that smirking face into the ground. In the meantime, could you please not give him any more reasons to gloat?"

"He gloats over something so trivial? Why this obsession with my hair?"

Finnian tugged at one of the bound locks. "I happen to like long hair. Gil says yours is almost to your waist."

She suppressed an instinctive laugh. "I suppose you'll find out after we're married." The morning's encounter flashed through her mind, forcing her to add beneath her breath, "If we're married."

"What was that?" the prince said.

"Nothing."

"Malena—"

"Have you seen Lili today?"

Confusion wrinkled his brows. "No."

Where had the creature gone? To the ocean steps, perhaps?

Magdalena's thoughts turned cynical. "*She* wears her hair down. Do you like it?"

He moved in close and kissed her just beneath her ear, sending a shiver through her. In a murmur he said, "I prefer brunettes. Sarcastic ones."

"Your Highness, some decorum, please," said Captain Byrne across the room.

"Shove off, Gil," said Finnian, settling back into the sofa.

His parents appeared shortly thereafter, and they proceeded to their meal. Magdalena, on edge for when or if the foundling would appear, barely touched her food. Afterward, the queen led her away for more dress fittings and decision-making.

Supper passed in a similar fashion. "Are you feeling all right?" the prince asked, noticing her unrest.

She twisted the napkin in her hands. "Yes."

"You're not having second thoughts, are you?"

She looked up sharply, her gaze meeting his. "No," she said, but the word had no certainty behind it.

"What's wrong? Are things happening too fast?"

Anxiety sparked through her. "Is it too fast for you?"

He scoffed. "As far as I'm concerned, we've been engaged since I was twelve. It's been far too slow."

"What?" said Magdalena. The prince at twelve meant she had been only ten years old. "That's rubbish. Back then you always talked about how you would have to bring your bride back from somewhere else."

"Well, of course. I knew my parents would send you away as soon as they caught on. That magic of yours preempted them. And I *would* have brought you back if my father hadn't done it first. But why do you look so thunderstruck? I told you I pined after you for years."

She swatted at him, too flustered to answer.

He grunted. "I can't visit you tonight. That hall they've put you in has half a dozen guards stationed in it all night long. I think that was by design."

"You think?" she asked, covering her disappointment with a wry smile. "Should I try climbing out my balcony?"

"Don't you dare. I won't have you breaking your neck."

"Then we'll have to forego this evening's tryst," she said. Although she wished it were otherwise, the new room and added guards would at least prevent her from waking with a malevolent sea-fay beside her.

Still, restlessness ate at her as she readied for bed. She slept with her ring on, and checked that it was still there the moment she awoke.

The days passed quickly with wedding plans and preparations. The Grand Duke and Duchess of Ondile arrived near the end of the week in a colorful entourage, with flowers and servants and boxes upon boxes of wedding gifts. Magdalena's mother enveloped her in a perfume-laden hug. Her father spent the afternoon with King Ronan and Prince Finnian, discussing what political arrangements a marriage between the two governments might necessitate. In a flash Magdalena shifted into her proper role as the daughter of nobility, complete with a personal maid and a dozen pastel dresses to choose from each day.

And Lili lurked at the edges of the commotion, silent and watchful, a silver shadow that slipped away whenever Magdalena spotted her. That creeping presence preyed upon her thoughts and disrupted her sleep.

If Finnian did not marry her, she would die.

But would Finnian *want* to marry her if he had not already chosen another?

The night before the wedding, Magdalena tapped on the infirmary door. Master Asturias looked up from his desk in the corner. "To what do I owe this visit?"

She held aloft the book of fairy lore, which had gotten jumbled with her own things amid the upheaval of changing rooms. "I've brought this back. Sorry it took me so long."

"Did you find the answers you sought?"

She hesitated, but the emotional misgivings within her pressed her to speak. "Yes and no. It says that fairies and humans sometimes marry, but that they're not compatible. But what if their lives are tied to one another already? What if… what if a fairy's life depended on a human's?"

He tipped his head. "How so?"

"Through a curse, perhaps?" The glamour that surrounded Lili, whether she had agreed to it or not, appeared to fall on that side of the magical spectrum.

"A curse that binds a fay to a human?" Master Asturias asked.

"Not binds, exactly. The fay's life becomes dependent on the human's."

Skepticism pulled at one corner of his mouth. "Fay and humankind are not meant to live together. That's why any treaties between the two realms have always failed. A fay whose life becomes dependent on a human's, for whatever reason, should accept its inevitable death. And vice versa."

Magdalena flinched. "But why?"

He stepped the distance between them and plucked the book from her hands. With stern expression he waved it at her. The faded golden letters upon its battered cover gleamed in the lantern light. "This told you, didn't it? When fay and humans join together, the children they produce are sterile. Such a union marks the end of their line. On a grander scale, it threatens the existence of each species. Everything in this world has its proper order. Fay belong with fay, and humans with humans. No magic is powerful enough to change that. It is a law, not a suggestion."

She considered this declaration, her heart still in turmoil. Master Asturias set the book on his examination table and patted her shoulder. She looked up into eyes that were surprisingly full of compassion.

"Marry your prince with a conscience free of guilt, Magdalena of Ondile," he said. "You cannot save that creature from the fate that awaits her. Brine and bone will always be brine and bone."

Her breath caught. He turned away, picking up the book again to replace it amid its fellows on the shelf.

"You knew?" she asked.

He did not even glance at her. "I surmised. Why do you think the king and queen were so frantic to draw their son's attention elsewhere?"

"Then the king and queen—"

"It's no use discussing it. All any of us can say aloud is that she really is the prettiest little thing."

He returned to his work without another word. Magdalena left the infirmary in a daze and traced the path back to her bedroom. As she neared, the strains of night music floated on the air, a lone violinist fiddling to the wind.

A hand grasped her arm and dragged her into a sheltered nook. "I hardly ever see you anymore," the prince said, holding her close. His teasing smile instantly shifted to concern. "What's wrong? Are you crying?"

She rested her head on his shoulder and let the gathering tears fall. "Just tell me everything will be all right."

Finnian cradled her, his cheek against her hair. "Of course it will. Shh, don't cry. You know I could never stand to see you cry."

"I have to," she said fiercely. "I have to!"

So he tucked her close and let her, whispering words of comfort all the while. Gradually the tension drained from her shoulders and the grief wrung from her heart. Tomorrow she would marry her love, and that act would cause another to die.

But stalling would not save Lili. The crown prince of Corenden could not end his family line by wedding a sea-fay, and even if he were so inclined, Magdalena could not bear to give him up.

Chapter Fourteen

THE BRIDE, RESPLENDENT in ivory silks and satins, floated through the chapel as though carried upon a cloud. The groom received her with a smile. Onlookers young and old shed tears—some of joy, and others of despair. The couple exchanged their vows and a kiss across the altar, and the priest presented them as the crown prince and princess of Corenden.

It happened so quickly, like a dream. Only Finnian's hand clasping her own anchored her to reality. Faces blurred amid the flower sprays that lined the chapel. At the far end of the room, a silver figure skirted out of sight.

The crowd moved from the church to the banquet hall, and then to the sheltered pavilion by the sea, where the breeze fluttered up from the ocean steps. Lili did not appear again until the bridal couple sat at the high table and the chamber orchestra began.

"We should go," Finnian said as the silver figure twirled into the room amid the other dancers.

Magdalena shook her head, her muscles tense, her feet in agony. "I want to stay."

His brows arched, and apprehension shot through his eyes.

She clasped his hand in quiet reassurance. "I feel as though I owe it to her to stay. Not all night, but long enough."

He tightened his fingers around hers. Together they watched the dance, Finnian solemn and Magdalena with forced serenity. Lili leapt and spun as though she were the soul of music itself. Her grace mesmerized the crowd and the intensity of her expressions—sorrow, rapture, despair—brought tears to their eyes.

The emotional overflow masked Magdalena's sheer agony. She freely wept, knives and daggers thrusting through her as she maintained her gentle smile.

She embraced the pain. She could not change the foundling's fate, but she could offer penance for her own part in sealing it.

The reeling music ended, and the dancers bowed upon the floor. Their audience applauded, and for Lili most of all. She raised her head, smiling, breathing deep, until her shining eyes fell on the bride and groom and clouded over.

"Is it long enough?" Finnian asked.

Magdalena, still battling the aftermath of such acute torture, managed a silent nod.

They rose together and took their leave amid toasts from their boisterous guests. Captain Byrne gave them both a mocking salute at the doors and made no attempt to follow. Magdalena, her legs still pricked by pins-and-needles numbness, hung upon her prince's arm all the way to his room, their bridal suite, where he promptly dismissed her maid and his manservant together.

"Do you think that's wise?" she asked, well aware of how trussed and tied she was into her dress.

"I think we'll manage on our own," he said with laughing, adoring eyes. "Let down your hair, Malena. I've waited long enough."

Chapter Fifteen

SHALLOW GRIEF PEPPERED HER DREAMS. The ladies of the court sobbed into their pillows in the early morning hours, after the party at the pavilion dissipated and the palace settled into silence.

He was supposed to belong to everyone, but if not, why her?

She shifted in her husband's arms and drowsily pushed her sensory magic another direction.

Sister. Sister, come home.

Buoyancy bobbed her up and down, up and down. The grief here ran deep like a throbbing wound. Half a dozen creatures clotted the base of the ocean stairs where a silver-haired figure huddled in misery. Their spiky heads glistened with water droplets beneath the sprawling starlight.

Sister, we traded our hair to bring you home.

The miserable figure raised her eyes to view the cluster. Webbed fingers lifted from the water, bearing a jagged knife.

End his life and you can return to the sea. Act quickly, before the sun appears.

The figure reached a delicate hand toward the slick hilt. As she brushed against it, the glamour upon her slipped. Torn webbing flashed into view. The hand drew back in surprise.

Quickly, sister. This will mend what was broken, blood for blood.

The silver foundling looked into the eyes of her pleading kindred. Her anguished heart yearned only to live. Resolved, she grasped the jagged dagger and the glamour fell away.

Magdalena awoke with a gasp, the bridal suite dim in the faint light of approaching dawn. She lay perfectly still, her eyes fixed on the wall, her ears listening to the silence as she considered the terrifying dream. An ocean breeze caressed her cheek. Beside her, Finnian shifted in his sleep, drawing her closer. His breath ghosted across the curve of her skin where her neck met her shoulders.

All was warm and quiet.

She released her pent-up tension in a sigh and rolled to look upon her sleeping husband—and froze.

A silver shadow loomed beside him: bulbous eyes and needle-sharp teeth, with long, brittle hair atop a noseless face. The sea-fay knelt upon the mattress. Magdalena's breath caught between her teeth as the gleam of a jagged knife flashed in the dimness.

Lili held it aloft, ready to plunge it into Finnian's chest.

"Don't." The word left Magdalena's lips on a tattered whisper. "Please, I beg you."

The sea-fay, terrifying in her forced silence, tipped her head to one side. Her marbled eyes regarded her human rival as though she couldn't quite grasp what she saw. She shifted her attention back to the sleeping prince, and her grip tightened on the knife.

End his life and you can return to the sea.

Desperation clawed up Magdalena's throat. She cast a protective arm over her husband to shield him from harm. "If it's a life you need, take mine. Please, let him live. I can't bear this world without him." Beneath her touch, the prince stirred.

Lili blinked, ponderously. She contemplated first Magdalena and then the knife. Her teeth parted, but no sound emerged.

Tears pricked Magdalena's eyes and her stomach clenched with terror. The wind blew through the open balcony doors behind the sea-fay, wafting the curtains inward and flooding the room with the scent of salt water.

End his life...

"Please," Magdalena said again.

The prince inhaled a deep breath. "Malena," he murmured in his fading sleep.

Lili jerked as though burned. She glanced from the prince to Magdalena and back again, water brimming in her huge eyes. A strangled, inhuman noise squeezed from her throat, and her face twisted with anguish. The knife raised high again.

Magdalena huddled against Finnian, covering his heart, exposing her own back to receive the fatal blow. She tucked her arms close and breathed the smell of his skin as she braced for death.

The inhuman noise sounded again, and agony flooded Magdalena's senses. In her periphery, the silver creature flung the dagger away. It skittered across the marble tile to the open doors, where it spun over the balcony's edge. For one horrifying moment, silence spread through the room. Magdalena stared into the wide, frightened eyes of the sea-fay.

In the distance, a low splash broke the trance. Half a dozen shrieks pierced the air. The foundling's feet hit the floor and pounded in a run, shooting phantom swords up Magdalena's legs. Pain blossomed in spots of dancing light as Lili bolted through the balcony doors and launched herself over the balustrade.

Magdalena cried out, half-raised to follow, but a hand clamped around her wrist. She looked down in shock and met the clear gray gaze of her husband. He said not a word.

From the sea below sounded a second splash.

Her magical senses exploded. She tore from the bed and across the room into the morning wind to hang upon the balcony. Far below, a patch of ocean shimmered blood-red in the gray light. Nearby, a silver figure floated on the water, the torn and angry flesh of her makeshift legs at ease in their native element. Shadows swam from the far-off reef, arms outstretched to retrieve the tattered body.

And the first rays of the dawning sun crested the horizon.

Lili's back arched. Her head dipped into the brine and her arms flailed out as her fingers and feet *dissolved*...

A sob caught in Magdalena's throat. The phantom void ate away at her limbs.

Brine and bone. Nothing but brine and bone, and a tiny scrap of soul.

Flesh decayed into foam. The bulbous eyes closed in docile acceptance of this fate. The converging shapes in the ocean halted, and the slick heads of six sea-fay surfaced, stricken, to gape at the awful transition from life to nothingness.

From above, the wind coursed down to the undulating waters, a funnel of energy centered upon that vanishing form. A thousand slender arms reached from within the gust, desperate fingers stretched taut. The water surged, and liquid met air to strip the mortal trappings away.

In the midst of this consuming death, the grasping wind enveloped a silver scrap of soul and lifted it to safety, dancing away into the clouds above.

Magdalena's knees buckled, her eyes fixed upon the sky as she hit the marble tile.

"It's over," Finnian said beside her.

She looked to him in wonder, oblivious to when he had joined her. He pulled her close and kissed her tear-streaked face.

"It's over, Malena," he said again. "She's gone to her rightful realm."

"No." Her voice wavered, barely discernible. "She's gone to a higher one."

And the swirling wind around them whispered its quiet confirmation while sunrise stained the clouds a glorious rose.

Epilogue

I SEE SO MUCH OF MY HUSBAND in our son: the same gray eyes, the same charming smile. He runs through the palace with joyful abandon, the pride of Corenden and Ondile both.

And wherever he is, a whispering breeze follows.

I dream of her often, the glamoured sea-fay who spared my husband's life not once, but twice. She dances through the clouds, her spirit exquisite in its ephemeral form, freed from mortal pain and grief. Sometimes I see her on the wind that curls around my child, amid a thousand other faces that whisper blessings as they pass. For an instant, their presence grows bright.

And then my eyes adjust and they are gone.

Master Asturias says that there are ancient tales of wind-children: neither human nor fay, but something in between. They glide the lengths of the earth seeking those good and kind souls that inhabit it, drawing strength from the goodness they find. And when they gather enough virtue to themselves, their own scrap of soul becomes complete and they continue into the next life as though they were whole and human all along.

A fanciful story, he says with his mouth at a cynical slant.

But I believe it.

When my husband wraps me in his arms, when our son plays among fluttering leaves and flowers, I believe it so strongly that my heart might burst.

The End

About the Author

Kate Stradling is the author of seven fantasy novels, including *Namesake, Goldmayne: A Fairy Tale, Kingdom of Ruses, Tournament of Ruses,* and *The Legendary Inge.* She received her BA in English from Brigham Young University and her MA in English from Arizona State. She blogs about linguistics, language use, and literary tropes at katestradling.com. She currently lives in Mesa, Arizona.

Made in the USA
Las Vegas, NV
14 December 2023

82768668R00100